LAST CHANCE

"I got no hankerin' to kill any of you folks. But I ain't going back. Not with a posse. You let things settle down and get folks back there to listen to some sense, and I'll come on my own. Till then, though, I expect you best head on back before someone gets hurt."

Burleson turned to his men and said something that Ramsey could not hear at his distance. Suddenly all the men in the posse spurred their horses forward.

"Hell and damnation," Ramsey muttered. He snapped the rifle up and pumped out six quick shots. The first two he deliberately put into the ground; the next four took down horses. He was still reluctant to shoot anyone, but he had to stop them and soon. They were within two hundred yards . . .

* * *

This book contains an exciting excerpt from *Six-killer* by Giles Tippette. Follow Justa Williams as he protects his family from a band of wild cut-throats on the Texas frontier! Available now from Jove Books.

PLAINS WAR

WILL McLENNAN

JOVE BOOKS, NEW YORK

PLAINS WAR

A Jove Book / published by arrangement with
the author

PRINTING HISTORY
Jove edition / May 1992

ISBN: 0-515-10848-0

Jove Books are published by The Berkley Publishing Group,
200 Madison Avenue, New York, New York 10016.
The name "JOVE" and the "J" logo
are trademarks belonging to Jove Publications, Inc.

PLAINS WAR

CHAPTER

★ 1 ★

Buck Ramsey chewed his lower lip as he looked at the sagging, painted signpost dangling between two warped logs embedded in the rolling prairie of east-central Colorado Territory. It said, simply:

BIG HORIZON RANCH

He sat on his horse, suddenly uncertain. He had traveled a long, hard road to be here, but now he was not sure he should proceed. It had been almost three years since he had seen Miss Eula Mae McFarrin. He could still picture that day. The beautiful Eula Mae riding off on the wagon with her grandmother, Maybelle Sweet, surrounded by her father's ranch hands for protection. And him riding off in the opposite direction, his seriously wounded brother, Matt, next to him. He had been torn then—desire to chase after Eula Mae caught up with worry about Matt.

That road had been a long, hard one, too, back then. He had been hired by Eula Mae's father, Artemis McFarrin, to take Eula Mae, Maybelle, Eula Mae's mother, Ada June, and her twin brothers, Lucius and Edgar, from Texas up here to the Big Horizon, McFarrin's new ranch. They had made it as far as the raucous, rambunctious, festering town of Justice, in the Indian Nations. Along the way, Ada June McFarrin had died, as had the ex-slave Jemma, Lucius, one of the twins, and both cowboys that McFarrin had sent along to help out Ramsey. There had been a running battle with Comanches, several run-ins with the two cowboys, encounters with drunken citizens of various two-bit towns, and more.

1

All in all, Ramsey realized, it was not a very pleasant memory. Except for the part with Miss Eula Mae McFarrin. Ramsey had declared his love for the golden-haired young beauty, and she for him. But after her mother had died, Eula Mae felt it only right that she should go on to the Big Horizon to run her father's household. She had made it clear that she wanted Ramsey to come around courting. And he had promised to do so.

But in the almost three years that followed, Ramsey had too often found himself caught up in one adventure after another with his brothers, Matt, Kyle, and, occasionally, Luke. He had always planned to stop by the Big Horizon, but somehow the opportunity had never presented itself, until now.

He and Luke had gone up into the mountains of Colorado Territory to visit Kyle. After clearing up some problems in Plentiful, Kyle decided it was time to return to the family homestead in Fannin County, Texas. They encountered a little trouble on the trail, but when that was taken care of, Buck had sat up one morning and realized how close he must be to the Big Horizon Ranch.

"I'm goin' on to see Miss Eula," he had announced that morning.

"Who?" Kyle asked, a twinkle in his eye.

Buck had explained. Then Kyle had nodded, understanding. He had had his own trials and tribulations with women, losing several to violence. He could understand his young brother's need.

Buck had ridden out that morning, heading eastward, out of the foothills of the Rockies and onto the rolling plains. Five days later he was sitting in front of the ranch sign, wondering if he should go on. Finally he snorted in disgust at himself and touched his spurs lightly to the sides of the ginger-colored horse.

He rode slowly down the meandering dirt road. In trying to keep his mind off the pending reunion, he wondered why the road had been built here. It seemed to go nowhere; it just ambled around grassy mounds and through dry, sometimes brushy coulees.

The ranch house suddenly popped into view about a hundred yards away as he rounded a bend in the road. He pulled up his horse and sat, taking in the sight. The house was two-story clapboard, painted a soft, gentle brown with white gingerbread trim. A wide, covered porch moved along the two sides Ramsey could see. He assumed it went all the way around the back and other side, too.

To Ramsey's left, set back from the road a few yards, sat a large wood barn. Behind it, a bit farther west, was a rickety corral. Ramsey wondered where McFarrin had gotten all the wood. Planking and logs were scarcer than hen's teeth out here on this generally treeless prairie.

A dozen or so horses that Ramsey could see stood in the corral, tails swishing lazily at flies. Across the yard from the corral and barn, forty or fifty yards away, backed up against a low ridge, sat a long, narrow bunkhouse. A sprawl of several towering cottonwoods indicated the presence of a spring or stream. Ramsey thought he could see a herd of cattle grazing way off to the north.

On the east side of the house was a large garden. Most of the crops were tall and brightly green, seemingly ready for harvesting. Ramsey liked to think Eula Mae had her hand in bringing such a thing to life. A line of trees just east of the garden, meandering toward him some yards off the road, hinted at a stream there.

Second thoughts began crowding into Ramsey's mind again. He was suddenly certain that Eula Mae would no longer be interested in him. He was certain she would be married by now. Three years was such a long time, and a young woman as vital, beautiful, and so full of life as Miss Eula Mae McFarrin would not go long unclaimed. It was too much, Ramsey figured, to think that she had waited around all this time just for him to show up. No, not too much, he corrected himself silently, it was a downright foolish notion.

He was on the verge of pulling his horse around and racing off, heading for Texas as fast as Biscuit could carry him. But he shrugged that off. He was a Ramsey. And, like all the Ramseys, was consumed by pride. He could not turn tail and run. He had set his course, and he would follow through on it. If Eula Mae did not want him, he would know that for sure, and could head for home with head held high. But to run now, after coming this far and without at least seeing Eula Mae, was too sickening for him to even consider.

Once more he touched the small silver rowels of his spurs to Biscuit's sides and moved on. He tried to blank out any worry from his mind as he rode those final yards toward the house.

He stopped near the porch, noting the spray of colorful flowers planted around it. He dismounted and tied Biscuit's reins to the hitching post just to the right of the porch steps leading to the front door. His mouth was dry. Never before had he felt such fright inside. Not through all the gunfights and Indian attacks and brawls and confrontations. He had grown considerably in the three years since he had seen Eula Mae—both in size and in maturity. He had killed more than his share of men, and had done plenty to right some pretty powerful wrongs. But now he suddenly was afraid. His knees felt weak and his palms damp.

He steeled himself and clumped up the four steps and across the porch. He rapped on the front door, noting almost unconsciously that there was real glass in all the windows of the house. McFarrin must be doing real well for himself, Ramsey thought, to be able to afford all this wood and real glass.

An old black woman opened the door. "Yassir?" she asked, disinterest written over her thin, wrinkled face.

"I come to pay my respects to Miss Eula," Ramsey said, cursing inwardly when his voice croaked from dryness and the worry that coursed through him.

"Yassir. Who I say be callin' fo' her?"

Ramsey's heart soared. She must not be married then if she was still living here. "Buck Ramsey," he said, his voice displaying more of his normal confidence.

"Wait inside heah," the woman said, stepping back to allow him to enter the dim hallway. She shut the door behind him and then shuffled off down the hallway.

Ramsey stood uncomfortably with his hat in hand looking around at the dim pictures and colorful, flowered wallpaper while he waited.

The black woman returned quickly. With a grumbled, "Follow me," she turned and shuffled off again. Ramsey followed. The woman stopped at a doorway and indicated with a wave of an arthritic old hand that he should enter.

Ramsey nodded thanks, shrugged, and walked into the room. His heart pounded in anticipation.

The disappointment he felt when he saw only Artemis McFarrin in the room was considerable. McFarrin had changed little since Ramsey had last seen him. He was still well-dressed in expensive clothes, and still wearing the same gold watch fob across the vest stretched by his stout middle. His hair, thick mutton-chops, and sagging mustache might be a little grayer, but not much.

McFarrin wore a dour expression as he stepped forward, hand outstretched. "Mr. Ramsey," he said with a not-altogether-friendly nod.

"Mr. McFarrin," Ramsey said warily as he shook the older man's hand.

"What brings you to the Big Horizon after all this time, Mr. Ramsey?"

McFarrin's voice was even, but Ramsey could sense the unfriendliness in the man. He was surprised by it. While he and McFarrin had had their troubles in the past, when they had parted, it was with at least a minimum of friendliness.

"I come to see Miss Eula," Ramsey said tightly.

"She's not here." McFarrin glared at Ramsey.

"Then where . . . ?" He stopped as Eula Mae bounced into the room. His heart seemed to surge up into his throat and his tongue suddenly seemed swollen.

She was as beautiful as he remembered. Maybe more so, considering she was now nineteen and had filled out a little more and matured. His eyes drank in the golden hair, lustrous blue eyes, the generous mouth.

"Buck!" Eula Mae gasped. Her delight flashed across her pale face.

Then, just as rapidly, it fled, leaving her looking stern, almost old. "What're you doin' here?" Eula Mae asked, seeming to stumble over the words. She tried to cover up her embarrassment by looking at the floor and then glancing out the window.

"I thought you might be glad to see me," Ramsey said lamely. His discomfort grew, as did his worry.

"Well, I . . ." Eula Mae clamped her lips shut and walked toward the window. She stood there staring out.

The silence grew, lengthening and thickening. Eula Mae looked out the window, Ramsey stared at her shapely back, and McFarrin glared at Ramsey. Finally Eula Mae turned. She seemed composed, though Ramsey thought he saw worry lurking in her eyes.

"It was nice of you to stop by, Buck," Eula Mae said. "But . . . But . . ." She sighed and suddenly looked close to tears. "But, well, my time's taken up by other matters now, Buck. I . . ."

"There somebody else?" Buck asked dully.

"Yes," Eula Mae whispered. It seemed pained.

Ramsey felt like his heart had been carved out, dropped on the floor, and then run over by a herd of cattle. But his face did not betray the emotions that churned inside him, other than taking on a granite cast. He nodded. "Then, if that's your final word . . . ?"

Eula Mae nodded. She was afraid to speak.

"We'd be obliged if you wasn't to come around again, Mr. Ramsey," McFarrin said softly.

Ramsey shrugged. He had no real intention of coming back here. He was not one to force his way in where he wasn't wanted. Still, he wasn't about to make a promise he might not be able to keep.

"Well," he said quietly, settling his hat on his head, "I expect I'll be moseyin' on. The best to you, Miss Eula." He almost choked on those last words. If there indeed was another man, he did not want to wish Eula Mae anything of the kind. He took one last look at the stubborn, headstrong young woman. Then he spun on his boot heel and walked swiftly out of the room, down the hall, and outside.

Ramsey climbed on his horse and moved out slowly. As he hit the road away from the ranch, he was set in his mind that he would just keep going. But something nagged at his mind. Something about his reception in the McFarrin house did not seem right. Something was wrong; something out of the ordinary was bothering Eula Mae and her father. He just knew it.

He stopped and turned in the saddle, looking back. Everything seemed serene. Behind the house, chickens clucked and cocks crowed; the soft lowing of cattle drifted over the rolling land; birds chirped and twittered. Ramsey wondered how anything could be wrong in such a pleasant setting.

But he was convinced that something *was* wrong, and that quite possibly Eula Mae was in danger. He nodded and rode on again. On the way in, he had spotted a sign for a town called Dirt Creek. He decided that a stay in Dirt Creek for a spell would be just the thing. That way he could keep an eye on the Big Horizon and maybe ferret out what was wrong here and set it to rights.

And, he thought ruefully, if Eula Mae did have another man and did not want him; if everything was all right here, well, then, he would ride on back to Texas, quietly and with little trouble.

He figured that he owed Eula Mae that. Himself, too. It *had* been a long road getting here. He hadn't risked his neck just to turn away now. He just hoped it would be worth it.

Only three days ago, he had been hunkered down in a copse on a teeny island in the Arkansas River, sweating from the heat, fear, and excitement.

Six colorful warriors—he took them for Cheyennes, considering the location and the way they rode—had galloped helter-skelter around his position.

CHAPTER

★ 2 ★

Ramsey had coerced Biscuit as deep into the brush as he could, hoping the animal would be safe. Ramsey knew it would be hell out here, miles from anywhere, if he was on foot and there were hostile Cheyennes roaming around. But it was the best he could do, and he hoped for the best.

Then he had slid into position behind a log, praying that the six Cheyennes didn't have any friends coming up from the other side of the river, behind him.

He was surprised to see only six Indians. It worried him, since he figured there must be others about. After a short while, though, he remembered hearing somewhere that Indians often went out on raids in small groups like this. He hoped that was the case now.

Ramsey slid his Winchester rifle up over the log after checking to make sure it was loaded. He rested it on the log while he made certain he had a box of shells handy. The Winchester was a .44/40 and used the same cartridges as his Colt side arm. It saved time and trouble in a crunch like this. The pistol would come in handy if the fighting got to be close up. Still, he was a far better shot with the rifle, and planned to use that as much as he could. Ramsey brushed beads of sweat off his forehead with the sleeve of his shirt. He pulled his hat off and dropped it on the log near his left hand. "Damn heat," he muttered.

The Indians were still riding back and forth over on the riverbank, which was several feet higher than the island he was on. It gave the Cheyennes another advantage. It might be a small advantage, but he had learned from much hard-won experience that any advantage could mean the difference between life and death in such a situation.

Ramsey pulled the rifle up to his cheek and sighted down the barrel at a young, copper-featured warrior. The Cheyenne's face was painted in bold stripes of blue and yellow, and he looked fierce.

Ramsey snicked back the Winchester's hammer and began to apply the slightest pressure on the trigger. Then he stopped himself. He moved his index finger carefully away from the trigger, and let his breath out slowly.

James Buchanan Ramsey had killed men before—far more than he thought was good for a man of such still-young years. After all, he was barely twenty. But while he had sent more than a few men to the Hereafter, he was not a born killer. He got no satisfaction from it, and certainly no joy. He simply did what he had to do.

Right now, he did not think he had to shoot down one of these Indians in cold blood, although it might, he realized, save some trouble—maybe even his life—if he did so. But it was not within him to do that. He would try to let the Cheyennes make the first move.

The afternoon began to drag on. The heat grew more fierce, and droplets of sweat dribbled from his thatch of straw-colored hair, down across his broad forehead, and dropped off his slightly beaked nose and broad, square chin.

The sweat he could take, he thought. But the damned mosquitoes, gnats, and other water-drawn insects—and the fear—made the waiting miserable. He used his hat to swat frequently, at times almost constantly, at the swarms of pesty insects.

"Come on, damn your hides," he mumbled softly after half an hour or so had passed.

After an hour, he was annoyed. He had never possessed all the patience of, say, his brother Luke, who found comfort in his Bible readings. This waiting was wearing on him. He had learned already that he was, much like Kyle and Matt, a man of action. This lying around waiting for something to happen was not for him.

Finally he smiled and raised the rifle again. He might not be a cold-blooded killer, but there was nothing to stop him from wounding an Indian. Or just sending a volley of shots out there at the Cheyennes. It might be enough to scare them off. Or make them charge. In which case he would be justified in dusting one or two of them. That would discourage the others for sure.

He slid the hammer back and sighted at another warrior. This one was a few years older. He had a hawklike face and a broad, flabby chest. Like the others, he was almost naked. They wore no war bonnets; simply some feathers tied in their hair. This one carried a Winchester rifle that had a broken stock. The wood had been repaired by wrapping some copper sheeting around the break and then tacking it down tightly.

Ramsey fired.

The warrior was almost flung to the ground as his horse bolted. With the rope rein snapped by Ramsey's bullet, the Indian had nothing to grasp, and he nearly went off over the back of the horse's rump. Only a supreme effort to jerk himself forward kept the Cheyenne seated.

Ramsey laughed at the sight of the fierce warrior scrabbling frantically to keep himself on the horse's back, seeking to grab the flapping mane, as the steed raced westward along the bank. "That'll teach him," Ramsey muttered.

He even felt some sense of relief when he heard the other warriors also laughing. The Indians shouted in their own language after their departed comrade, hooting and jeering. Though Ramsey could not understand a single word of what they were saying, he knew they were ribbing their companion.

Twenty minutes or so later, though, he was growing annoyed at the heat and the insects once again. The Cheyenne warrior returned about then. Ramsey could tell even at this distance that his face was twisted in a fierce scowl. He growled something at his companions, who laughed some before sobering.

Ramsey found that he was having trouble staying awake, despite the insects that seemed determined to reduce him to a pile of bleaching bones.

But the screech of a Cheyenne war cry and a short, sharp volley of gunfire aimed in his direction served to snap him alert. "Damn, damn," he whispered. He had glanced up and seen all six Cheyennes charging down the riverbank and splashing into the water. All were firing their rifles.

Ramsey ducked behind the log as branches, leaves, twigs, and chunks of wood flew by him, chewed down by the gunfire. He reached up, grabbed the butt of his rifle, and slid it quickly toward him. Then he rolled to his left several times, jerking the lever of his rifle up and down as he did.

He finally came to a stop six feet from where he had been, but still behind the log. He popped his head and the rifle over the wood and fired twice before he even really looked. He had precious little to aim at, as the Indians had slid off the sides of their horses and were galloping along through the shallow water, using their horses as shields.

For an instant, Ramsey considered shooting the horses, putting the Cheyennes afoot. But he decided he could not do that. Not yet, anyhow. He had spent much time catching and breaking horses with his brother Matt, and so had too much respect for good horses to do such a thing lightly.

Ramsey jumped up and then dived for the cover of a bush a few feet to his left, beyond the old root ball of the fallen tree. He landed on a sharp branch or root, bounced, and came to a halt. Pain stabbed through his side from where it had hit the branch. Ramsey looked down quickly and saw that there was no blood. He pushed himself up and ran through the thicket.

He angled around, wanting to head back toward the log, and more importantly, Biscuit. He heard the Indians splashing out of the river and riding slowly past where he had been a few moments ago. He stopped, breathing hard from the run and the pain in his side. But he knew he could not let them know where he was by crashing around like a wounded buffalo.

He stood, bent over, holding his rifle across his thighs. He tried to suck in air quickly but silently. He wasn't sure he was entirely successful. He listened as the Indians moved along, probing the brush, looking for him.

That's when he really began to worry. For one thing, the Indians were close enough that with the brush, any encounter would force Ramsey to use his pistol. For another, with the Indians here on the island, they could not help but find Biscuit sooner or later. And if they did, they might just take the horse and ride off, leaving him afoot. He didn't like this one little bit.

He straightened. He would have to accept the situation as it stood, and work within its constraints. With his rifle in his left hand, leaving his right free to go for the pistol on his hip if necessary, he once more began working his way toward Biscuit. But this time he walked slowly, trying to be as quiet as he could. Despite his footsteps, he could still hear the Cheyenne ponies.

Brush tore at his clothes as he forced his way through another thicket. Suddenly he burst through the confining closeness of a bush and found himself in a small, angular clearing.

And staring at a young, war-painted but otherwise pleasant-looking Cheyenne warrior.

Time seemed to stand still for the two men. The wind ruffled trees and brush, creating a soft, rustling sound. The hoof steps of

Indian ponies could be heard quietly not far away. Birds chirped softly once again.

"I don't suppose it'd do any good for me to ask if you and your friends'd be willin' to make a peace here and go our separate ways?" Ramsey mentioned, a note of hope in his voice.

"You're afraid," the warrior said in good English. That surprised Ramsey.

" 'Course I'm afraid," Ramsey said quietly. He showed no fear, though he felt it. He had been in worse positions before, and so wasn't too concerned. Yet.

"All white-eyes are afraid," the Cheyenne boasted.

"Shit," Ramsey muttered. A sneer curled his lips. "I suppose you ain't?" He looked up at the Indian, who still sat on his horse. He held a Henry repeating rifle in his hands, and there was a big six-shooter in a holster that dangled from the saddlehorn of a Cavalry saddle.

"No." The Indian's voice was full of disdain.

"You should be."

The warrior spit in disgust. He had been insulted and thought it time to teach this impudent white-eyes a lesson he would take to his grave. With a sneer, he began swinging his Henry rifle up.

Ramsey hesitated not an instant. He jerked out the new .44-caliber Colt Army pistol he had bought about a year ago. He snapped off two quick shots. He had never been as good with a pistol as he was with the Winchester, but he had always managed to get by.

The Cheyenne's shot went wild as two slugs from Ramsey's Colt ripped into his stomach and chest. Shock flickered in his eyes momentarily, until death clouded the almost black orbs. He fell off his horse with a thud. The pony skittered away nervously.

Ramsey knelt, resting the Winchester against one knee. In moments he had ejected the two spent shells from the pistol and replaced them with fresh ones. He shoved the Colt into his holster, grabbed the Winchester, and took off running, into the brush once again. Already he could hear the other Cheyennes heading in his direction.

He skidded around a sugarberry tree and stopped. Through the screen of brush, he could see two warriors enter the small clearing almost at the same time, but from different directions. It worried him that three were still out there under cover somewhere. He shrugged and moved off again, quickly but mostly silently.

He slowed and took more caution as he neared his ginger-colored stallion. As he approached, he thought he saw a movement near the animal. He held his breath and crept forward.

It was instinct more than anything else that made him duck his head. It was the only thing that kept him alive, since the Indian war club whistled within an inch of smashing his temple. Instead, it just glanced off the side of his head. He fell, not hurt too badly, but propelled by his ducking motion and the added urging of the war club. He dropped the Winchester when he hit the ground, but he caught himself on his arms, spun, and kicked the Cheyenne's feet out from under him.

The Indian went down like a poleaxed steer, grunting when his rear end hit the dirt.

Ramsey shoved himself over so he could get at the Army Colt. He yanked it out and fired. The bullet tore off part of the Indian's left ear. His second shot was more accurate, and hit the Cheyenne in the face.

Ramsey scrambled up and shoved his pistol away. He looked around worriedly, trying to find his Winchester. He spotted it, scooped it up, and shoved it into the saddle scabbard on Biscuit. He took a moment to think of his choices. But his only choice was clear.

He leaped into the saddle and spurred Biscuit through the heavy brush, racing off. He charged into the river, slapping the horse with the reins. As Biscuit lurched up the riverbank, Ramsey glanced back over his shoulder. One of the Cheyennes was kneeling on the shore of the island, rifle raised. Ramsey didn't hear the shot until a second or two after he saw a bullet kick up a chunk of dirt off to his left.

Over the lip of the bank, Ramsey lashed the horse again and took off. Several times in the next couple of miles, he stopped briefly to look behind him. But there was no pursuit. After a half-day of mostly hard riding, he finally let the ginger slow to a walk. He made a cold camp that night, but by the next day he figured pursuit was not going to come. He relaxed.

Two days later, he was looking at the sign leading to the Big Horizon Ranch, wondering if he should proceed. But, after all he had been through to get here, he was not about to turn back now.

CHAPTER

★ 3 ★

Dirt Creek was a squalid little town with a severe case of delusions of grandeur. It was not very big, but it rambled over several acres. What passed for a main street was a hole-filled, wide dirt rut in the land that seemed to drift aimlessly hither and yon until there were no more buildings on either end. A few what might have been other streets entered it haphazardly from either side.

The buildings were sod and mud, maybe adobe. Some were covered with wood facades. Four actually were made of wood, with glass in the windows, and two were of brick. But they were by far in the minority. It was a sad, forlorn-looking town, though the people certainly seemed to be putting a good face on for the world.

As he rode in, Buck Ramsey noted the hovels that passed for houses and businesses. It meant little to him that Dirt Creek was such a poor-looking place. He had seen, and been in, far worse towns. Places like Justice, down in the Indian Nations, and a dozen others. This one, he thought, at least gave the appearance of trying to be a respectable town.

The wind was whipping up, and clouds covered the sky as he tied off Biscuit at the hitching rail in front of one of the few wood buildings. It also was one of the only two two-story buildings in Dirt Creek, the other being the bank, catty-corner to the hotel. The bank had the distinction of being one of the only two brick buildings in town. A sign proclaimed the hotel to be Wohlford's Hostelry and Chop House. It looked good to Ramsey after so many days on the trail. He slid his Winchester from the saddle scabbard and held it in his left hand. He pulled his saddlebags off and slung them over his left shoulder.

13

Soft droplets of rain began to splatter down as Ramsey entered the hotel. The lobby was plainly appointed with a worn carpet, dull draperies, and little furniture. An unadorned counter sat across the room. Behind it was a simple rack of small boxes for keys and what messages people might receive. A tall, potbellied man stood behind the counter.

The hotel owner was dressed in an immaculate white shirt, a crisp brocade vest, and almost-creased trousers. His hair was greased back, with one fancy spit curl plastered to his forehead. A trim, pencil-thin mustache was his only facial hair.

"Help you?" he asked, looking with distaste at Ramsey's worn outfit. Ramsey's clothes were bloody and covered with trail dust. His shirt was torn in many places from the brambles in the thicket on the island in the Arkansas. His boots were coated with old mud. His hat was soiled and had a bullet hole through the crown.

"I'd like a room," Ramsey said calmly, though a touch of anger flickered inside. He had some suspicions on what the man was thinking, and he did not like it. He rubbed a hand across the stubble on his chin, trying to stem the anger before it built too much. He knew he must look a fright. Still, he didn't think the man had to look down his nose at him because of it.

"How long?" The man's surly tones had not lessened any.

Ramsey shrugged.

"Fifty cents a night." He said it as if he believed his visitor didn't have enough for one night, let alone more.

Ramsey nodded. He reached into a pocket and pulled out a double eagle. "Put me down for a week," he said, an angry note brushing out with the words.

The hotel man looked at the bright gold coin suspiciously, as if he thought Ramsey might have made it materialize out of thin air.

"You do have change for it, don't you?" Ramsey asked sarcastically.

"Of course," the man said, flustered. He looked Ramsey over, taking in the Winchester, the well-worn, though well-cared-for Colt, and Ramsey's big size and hard look. He decided that his visitor had come by the money more or less honestly—probably by taking on some gunfighting job. He shrugged mentally. Such men had passed through Dirt Creek before, and undoubtedly would again.

"Good," Ramsey said. The sarcasm escaped the hotel man this time, though.

"First floor?"

"Second, if one's available," Ramsey said. He had learned that living on the first floor often was not safe. Should anyone decide to come looking for him—he really didn't expect that here, but one could never tell—that person would have to climb some steps and break into his room rather than just put a shot through a ground-floor window.

"Think I got one."

"Good," Ramsey repeated. "Can you have a tub sent up, with hot water? I expect I could use a bath."

"I expect," the man said dryly.

Ramsey was irritated at the man, since he was not sure the man was referring to his need for a bath or whether he was acknowledging that a tub and hot water were available.

"Sign here," the man said, turning the register book around to face Ramsey and holding out an inked pen. He looked up and asked, trying to seem innocent, "You do know how to write your name, don't you, boy?"

The hotel man blanched at the hard look that suddenly leapt into Ramsey's glittering blue eyes.

Ramsey managed to keep his temper in check. "Yep," he said evenly. "I can cut my own meat and make water all by myself, too."

The hotel man laughed brittlely a moment in nervous relief as Ramsey took the pen and scratched his name in the book. The hosteler turned the book back and glanced down at the name. "What're you doing in Dirt Creek, Mr. Ramsey?" he asked. "If you don't mind my asking."

"I do," Ramsey said coldly. It always amazed him when he spoke to a person in such a way. He had been brought up to be polite and to treat others kindly. But he was no longer a boy, and he had seen too much violence and hardship. He also had learned that some people did not deserve much courtesy. It was, he acknowledged, easier for him these days to be gruff with folks, even with well-meaning buffoons like this one.

The man cleared his throat nervously.

"You have me at a disadvantage now, too, mister," Ramsey said.

"Eh?"

"You got a name?"

"Ah, yes. Floyd Wohlford."

Ramsey nodded. "My room, Mr. Wohlford?"

"Of course." Wohlford was more flustered than he could ever remember being, and he was not sure why. Granted, Buck Ramsey was a hard man, and looked like he knew how to use the Colt Army on his hip. But other such men had not flustered him so. He turned, pulled a key out of a box behind him, and then placed it on the counter. "Room twenty-two. Upstairs at the back."

Ramsey nodded. He picked up the key.

"I'll have the tub sent up directly. Got me two darkies for such things." He smiled, pride evident on his face that he was rich and important enough to have such help. "They ain't the best, mind you, the lazy bastards," he added, almost in confidence. After all, he was talking with a fellow Southerner, one who would know and understand these things. "But they do all right, if you keep after 'em."

Buck Ramsey was not much of one for such talk. Never had been. None of the Ramseys were. Old Samuel and Alice Ramsey had not taught their sons and daughters such ways, and none had seen fit to pick them up. Even Matt and Kyle, who had fought for the South in the Cause, had not returned with such attitudes.

Ramsey knew, however, that such thinking was prevalent among many, and he knew there was no changing people. So he kept his mouth shut. He just nodded. "There a livery in town?"

Wohlford gave him directions.

"Can I trust him?" Ramsey asked suspiciously.

"Em Fortney's the most honest man in town. Ain't too smart, but honest as the day is long."

Ramsey nodded. "General store?"

"Simms's. Over yonder, next to the bank." He pointed. "You can't miss it."

"Obliged." Ramsey marched up the stairs to his room. It was more comfortably set up than he would have imagined. The bed looked inviting, though it was still early afternoon. Ramsey smiled at that. He dropped his saddlebags on the floor in a corner and headed out. As he was passing through the door, two black men neared. The young men were carrying a small copper tub.

Ramsey stepped back out of the way, holding the door for them. The act surprised the blacks considerably. The one, a little bigger than the other, nodded appreciatively.

"I'll be back directly, boys," Ramsey said. "So you can take your time fillin' that tub." He grinned, as if inviting the two to join him in a conspiracy against Wohlford.

The blacks grinned back, still confused. Ramsey's Texas accent gave him away as a Southerner, and that perplexed them. But Ramsey certainly seemed friendly enough. Still, they would be cautious around this man, for a while at least.

"Yassir," the one who had nodded before said.

Still with his Winchester in hand, Ramsey headed downstairs and outside into the splattering rain. He climbed onto Biscuit and rode slowly down to the livery stable.

As promised, Em Fortney was a dim-looking individual. He had an elongated, bony face and a concave chest. But he appeared friendly enough, and he looked over Biscuit with a practiced eye when Ramsey turned the ginger-colored horse over to him.

"Looks hard-used, Mr. Ramsey," Fortney said.

"Him and me, both," Ramsey said with a smile.

Fortney's head bobbed up and down, like a sunflower in the wind. "I'll treat him good, don't you fret," he said, head still pumping. "Make him good's new you leave him here long enough." He looked at Ramsey with a question in his walleyes.

Ramsey shrugged. "I'll be around a few days. Maybe more."

"Should be enough. Plenty of oats and hay. Restin' time." He walked away, leading the horse, still talking though he no longer had an audience.

Ramsey walked away, shaking his head at the strange stalk of a man. He headed through the steadily increasing rain, that was pushed now by a blustery wind, to Simms's store.

The general store was also a wood building, and it offered welcome relief to Ramsey. Without much fanfare, Ramsey quickly bought a new pair of denim trousers, a cotton shirt, a pair of longhandles, socks, a hat, and a slicker. He had lost his slicker somewhere along the trail in the past month or so, and with the rain coming down as it was, he decided one would come in handy. He paid for his purchases and walked out with the paper-wrapped package in hand.

One of the two young black men was pouring water into the tub as Ramsey entered his room. The other was rooting through Ramsey's saddlebags. He looked up guiltily when Ramsey stepped into the room.

Ramsey had the package and his Winchester in his left hand, so with his right hand he swept the Colt out of the holster. "Mind tellin' me just what you're doin' there?" he asked tightly. The Colt covered the one holding his saddlebags. It was the one who had spoken before.

"I . . . I . . ." The black man grinned and shrugged, trying to look innocent.

Ramsey thumbed back the Colt's hammer. The black began to sweat. Out of the corner of his left eye, Ramsey watched the other black. "I don't take kindly to thieves, sir," Ramsey said harshly. He paused. "No matter who that man is."

The black believed him, though he was scared half to death. He knew Ramsey could easily kill him, and, worse, would get away with it. There would be no one in Dirt Creek who would think anything of a white man killing a black man, especially one rifling through his property.

"You got anything to say for yourself?"

"No, sir." The young man looked abashed and afraid.

"You take anything?"

"No, sir." He held out his hands, showing what he was holding. He had a money pouch in one hand, and a straight razor in the other. "Ain't had time to take nothin'."

"What's your name?"

"Cyrus. Cyrus Douglas."

"Well, Mr. Douglas," Ramsey said, relaxing fractionally, "what am I gonna do about this?"

"I'd be obliged was you to fo'get about it," Douglas said quietly. He tried to smile but could not. He was ashamed at having been caught. But more, he was ashamed at having even tried to do this to someone who had treated him decently.

"You gonna try somethin' like this again?"

"No, sir."

"I'd like to believe that, Mr. Douglas."

Douglas could not believe this white Texan had called him "mister" twice in a matter of moments. He licked his lips nervously. "My word," he said quietly.

Ramsey hesitated only a moment. Something in the young man made him want to believe him. And he thought he could understand why Douglas had done what he did. Ramsey eased the hammer down. "Reckon that's good enough for me," he said. As he slid the Colt away, he added, "Now, suppose you put my things back." He indicated the money pouch and razor with a wave of his hand. "And you and your partner there can finish fillin' that tub."

"Yassir." Douglas's relief was palpable.

CHAPTER

★ 4 ★

The Red Dog was about the poorest excuse for a saloon that Ramsey had ever seen in his short life. It was, he admitted as he walked inside, a step or two above some of the festering sinkholes in Justice. But that wasn't saying much.

The saloon had rotting wood sides, but the roof was tenting canvas. The lanterns were smoky and dim, but enough of the daylight flooded in through the cracks in the wall to help out. The bar itself was a long, thin sheet of rusted tin nailed to several barrels. Ramsey found out later that the old beer barrels were filled with sand, both to make them too heavy to move, and to provide the bartenders some protection from flying bullets. There was no real back bar, just some crates piled atop each other. The crates were filled with bottles and jugs. A cash register sat inside one wood box.

The saloon was, however, open twenty-four hours a day, and seemed to be doing a sprightly business. Working women plied their trade, gambling wheels spun, and cards were dealt. The beer was plentiful, and almost cold, and the whiskey not watered down more than was usual for such a place.

Ramsey, Winchester in hand, clomped to the bar. He rested the rifle on the tin and ordered a mug of beer. When it was brought and paid for, he picked up the rifle in one hand and the beer in the other. He strolled away, looking for a place to sit. He finally found a smaller table toward the back that was empty. He set the beer and Winchester down on the sturdy table and sat in the rough chair.

He had been in Dirt Creek two days and was bored to death with it already. The people were friendly enough, but to Ramsey they seemed somewhat condescending, as if he wasn't good enough for the place. Beyond that, the place offered little in the way of amenities. He had visited what passed for a brothel twice already. The place was as poor as the Red Dog. The girls were, for the most part, rough, unattractive, and prone to churlishness.

As he sat, feet up on the table, beer in hand, resting on his stomach as he leaned back, Ramsey had half convinced himself that he would leave in a day or so, unless something happened concerning Eula Mae. On the other hand, he thought, he had made no effort to get back out to the Big Horizon Ranch to see what he could learn about the situation. He still suspected there was something wrong at the McFarrin place, something that meant trouble for Eula Mae and her father.

He considered riding out there now, since it was barely after noon, but he was feeling lazy. He finally decided that he would ride out to the McFarrin place in the morning and just nose around some. He would keep an eye peeled around the place, and see what he could learn. Maybe nothing, he knew, but he had nothing better to do. And, Lord knew, he might even end up learning something.

Ramsey also decided that he would give it three more days—three days of riding over the ranch land, poking his nose in where it might not be wanted. If he hadn't found out anything by then, he would head for home. After that long, he figured it should be apparent whether there was something bothering the McFarrin family or whether Eula Mae just didn't want him around anymore.

With his mind made up, he could relax mentally. He ordered another beer and settled back down to watch the world go by.

One of the more interesting characters in view was a burly, hatchet-nosed fellow sitting nearby. It was evident just by a glance that the man was a bully. He was filling up on liquor and losing steadily at faro. Both were making him steadily angrier. Ramsey smiled as he listened to the man's blustery snarls.

Ramsey's attention shifted from the man when one of the working girls strolled up to his table.

"Mind if I sit?" she asked wearily.

Ramsey shrugged, but he smiled. He had no desire for this woman. She was tall, raw-boned, and had a mouthful of crooked teeth. An altogether unpleasing looking specimen. Still, he was too polite to just send her away. She looked tired and worn out by her hard life, and he felt a short rest sitting here doing nothing might help her out some.

The woman sat. "I'm Daisy," she offered, passing off what she believed to be a smile.

"Buck. Want a drink?"

"Be nice."

They ordered her a drink. Neither said anything as they just sipped at their respective drinks. While doing so, Ramsey kept half an ear on the obnoxious man at the faro table. He was getting annoyed with the man.

Soon, Ramsey ordered another drink for Daisy. When she had finished that one, she said brusquely, "Well?"

"Well, what?" Ramsey asked. He wore an innocent expression.

"You comin' out back with me or not?"

"Reckon not."

Anger flashed across her face. "You mean I set here with you all this time for nothin'?" she demanded.

Ramsey shrugged and half grinned. "Thought I was doin' you a favor, lettin' you sit and rest a spell."

"Well you ain't. A girl's got to make some cash you know, and I ain't gonna make none settin' here watchin' you guzzle beer."

Ramsey shrugged again. "Didn't realize you was so anxious to throw yourself at a man." Such women bothered him more than a little.

"Well, I sure as hell ain't anxious to throw myself at you, buster," the woman snarled. Her already repugnant face curled up into a mask of truly incredible rancidness. "I ain't got time for any man ain't got the stones."

Ramsey colored at the insult. "I got the stones," he snapped back, just as angrily. "But I aim to save myself for a *woman*." He emphasized the last word.

Daisy opened the wide slash of her almost lipless mouth, as if to retort. But she had been in her business long enough to heed the warning signs of anger on a man's face. Especially a man as big as this one. He might be young, she thought, but he was well above average in size. She almost regretted having been so short with him, he probably would have been interesting to dally with for a spell. But it was too late for that now. She had to make some money, and it was apparent that she wasn't going to make any with this fellow. She settled for snarling, "Bah." She dismissed him with a wave of her hand and slumped off, big, flat feet slapping the dirt floor of the saloon.

Ramsey took a few moments to rid himself of the anger. But then he smiled. Daisy had been a feisty one, that was for sure. Not that he liked her any the better now, but at least she had provided something of a distraction. A small entertainment for a small-minded town.

Men were leaving the faro table, irked at the blustery man's oaths and growling. It began to annoy Ramsey. He hated to see people backing off from a bully. He considered joining the game himself, just to put the man in his place. But then he decided he didn't want to expend the effort. He leaned back and sipped beer.

He was near ready to leave when he heard the bartender shout, "Hey, you niggers know you ain't supposed to be in here." His voice carried over the normal din of the saloon, which began to quiet.

"But Mistah Cavanaugh, we's come . . ."

"Don't sass me, boy," Cavanaugh said arrogantly. "Just haul your asses out of my saloon. Both of you." He softened a little. "Go on, git, boys."

"But Mistah Cavanaugh . . ." Cyrus Douglas said, a note of pleading in his voice.

"No buts, Cyrus," Cavanaugh said. His voice was a mixture of barely held tolerance and anger. He had nothing against Cyrus Douglas and his companion, Solomon Jackson, but they were not supposed to be in this place, and he had to think of his reputation among the people of Dirt Creek.

"These niggers botherin' you, Cavanaugh?" a man asked.

Ramsey looked up to the see the burly, obnoxious faro player lurching toward Douglas and Jackson.

"This ain't your concern, Skinner."

"Shit, I ain't doin' so well at your rigged faro game. Might's well have *some* fun." His words were slurred, but he seemed competent enough as he turned toward Douglas and Jackson. "So, what say you boys fetch your asses a little closer so's I can whomp you without havin' to work up a sweat."

"I'll take care of this, Skinner," Cavanaugh snapped. "If your luck's bad at the faro table, that's no reason to stick your nose in where it don't belong." He looked a little worried. Clete Skinner was a mean enough man even when sober. When drunk and angry at having lost a bundle of cards, he would be downright ornery.

"Standin' here arguin' with these two niggers ain't taking care of the problem, Cavanaugh," Skinner said. His voice was condescending.

"Now, wait a minute, goddamnit, I . . ." Cavanaugh started.

He shut up in a hurry and ducked as Skinner pulled his pistol and fired without looking in Cavanaugh's general direction. Then Skinner turned the gun on the two young black men.

"Only thing I got to decide now," Skinner said coldly as he thumbed back the hammer of his Remington pistol, "is which one of you darkies I'm gonna shoot first." He began to grin, then started to laugh. "And jus' *where* I'm gonna shoot you."

The pistol moved from one to the other of the black men, who sweated with some fear. Douglas looked the calmer of the two, but he knew he was in deep trouble. Skinner had a hard reputation in town, and Douglas knew neither he nor his friend had any chance of justice in Dirt Creek, even if they could manage to get out of this.

The Remington seemed to settle on Douglas, at a point between knee and ankle. "Reckon I'll jus' start with you, boy," Skinner breathed.

His finger eased back from any pressure on the trigger as he felt a rifle barrel nearly lodge in his left ear.

"I'd not recommend that," Ramsey said icily.

"Who's that?" Skinner asked gruffly. Sweat popped out on the sides of his head, and the smell of fear and whiskey was heavy on him.

"The man's gonna plant your ass in the ground you don't put that piece away in a mighty goddamn big hurry."

"You might be advised, mister, whoever you are, that I don't take kindly to nigger-lovers." It was said in blustery tones and with a sense of self-confidence. Having Clete Skinner angry at you was enough to chill most men's bones in Dirt Creek.

"I don't see as you got much to say about it at the moment," Ramsey said calmly. "Now, point that Remington up at the sky and very carefully eject all the shells in it."

"If I don't?" Skinner inquired. He began to feel real fear now.

"Even a man's dumb as you can't be that goddamn stupid." Ramsey had not moved the rifle from Skinner's ear.

Very slowly Skinner lifted the pistol till the muzzle was straight up. He eased the hammer down. Then, afraid to move too much, he brought his left hand up and used it to work the ejector. Shells clinked on the dirt floor.

When Skinner's gun was empty, Ramsey said, "Holster it."

Skinner did as he was told. Ramsey carefully let the hammer of his Winchester down. Skinner began to relax. He opened his mouth and oaths aimed at Ramsey spat out.

Ramsey calmly held the rifle in both hands—left up on the barrel, right at the lever. He swiftly stepped in front of Skinner and snapped the weapon up. The butt broke Skinner's jaw.

Skinner shut up immediately as his jaw began to operate improperly. It took several seconds to realize that. When he did, anger and pain dulled his eyes.

"That's for insultin' me," Ramsey said quietly. He turned his back to Skinner. Suddenly he jerked the Winchester backward. The butt jammed hard and deep into Skinner's stomach.

Skinner's air whooshed out, and he doubled over, hands clutching his midsection.

"That's for insultin' these two boys and Mr. Cavanaugh," Ramsey said, still evenly. "And this," he added, "is just 'cause you're so goddamn ornery." He stepped back a pace or two and then snap-kicked Skinner in the face.

Skinner groaned through his smashed jaw and toppled over backward. He landed hard, small moans drifting out of his mangled mouth and aching belly.

Ramsey faced the two black men. "You all right, Cyrus? Solomon?"

"Yassir," Douglas answered for both.

"Good." He sighed. "Now, did you two have a reason to come in here? Cavanaugh's within his rights to keep you out less'n' you got business here, I expect." He didn't like it much, but there was little he could do to change either the saloon owner's thinking, or the law.

"Yassir," Douglas answered. "We come lookin' fo' you. We . . ." His eyes suddenly grew very wide. "Mistah Ramsey!" he yelled, pointing.

CHAPTER

★ 5 ★

Ramsey whirled, crouching and bringing up the Winchester as he did.

Skinner was propped up on one elbow. His Remington was still in the holster, but he had produced another, smaller pistol from somewhere. Ramsey did not hesitate. He snapped the Winchester's hammer back and fired from the hip. Then he swiftly levered another round into the chamber.

It was not necessary, though. Skinner had a bloody hole through his chest and was flat on his back. Ramsey was only worried that the dead man's twitches might cause him to fire the pistol.

Because of that, Ramsey hurriedly took the four steps to Skinner. He placed a boot on Skinner's wrist, and then bent and pulled the pistol free. He uncocked it and tossed it to Cavanaugh. The bartender caught it clumsily, almost dropping it in his nervousness.

Masking his annoyance at these events, Ramsey turned and walked back to Douglas and Jackson. The two were standing, mouths agape. "Well?" Ramsey demanded gruffly.

"Well what, suh?" Douglas asked, tearing his eyes away from the body and turning them on Ramsey. He looked at Ramsey with a new respect. And new fear. Douglas was maybe six inches shorter than Ramsey's six-foot-two or so, but he was broad of shoulder and back. He had long, powerful arms and a well-muscled neck. He could hold his own against most men, when pressed to it, but he began to think he would have little chance in a fight with Buck Ramsey.

"Well," Ramsey said slowly, trying not to let his exasperation out, "you said you come lookin' for me. Why?"

25

"Oh, yassir," Douglas collected himself. "We was sent here to fetch you."

"By who?" Ramsey's patience was wearing thin.

"Miz Maybelle."

"Maybelle Sweet?" Ramsey asked. The name gave him a lift. He had not seen the old woman—Eula Mae's grandmother—when he had been out to the ranch the other day, and he had wondered about her. He liked the feisty old woman. He would like to see her again.

"Yassir," Jackson answered. It was the first time Ramsey had ever heard the young man speak. He seemed to have not all his wits about him. He reminded Ramsey of a bull—strong, plodding, stupid, but also loyal and forgiving. Ramsey suspected the man stayed quiet most of the time around Douglas because it appeared Douglas had some book learning.

"Well, what's she want?" Ramsey demanded.

"To see you."

"Why?"

Douglas shrugged. How could he be counted on to know such things? All he knew was that the old woman had stopped by Wohlford's hotel and asked for Ramsey. When she found out Ramsey was not there, she paid Douglas and Jackson a dime each to find Ramsey and tell the Texan she wanted to talk to him. So here they were.

Ramsey nodded. Of course Maybelle would not have told these two anything more than necessary. There was no reason to. "Well, where is she, then?"

Before Douglas or Jackson could answer, Sheriff Woody Burleson strolled in. He was short and thin, but wiry. He had a huge cigar clutched between his teeth. He talked around it when he bellowed, "I heard there was a shootin' here." His voice was far louder and much deeper than one would have suspected, looking at the size of the lawman.

"Clete Skinner bought it, Sheriff," Cavanaugh said. He seemed a little dazed.

"That his piece there?" Burleson asked, pointing at the pistol Cavanaugh still held.

"One of them."

"What happened?" Burleson sidled up to the bar and rested his roostery elbows on the tin.

As Cavanaugh began to explain, Ramsey turned to the two young men. "You boys best haul out of here before the law starts askin' too many questions." He pulled a fifty-cent piece from his pocket and handed it to Douglas. "You best be sure you share this with Solomon, you hear?"

When Douglas had nodded excitedly, Ramsey asked, "Now, where's Miz Maybelle?"

"Said she'd wait fo' you at Mistah Simms's sto'," Douglas said.

"Thanks. Y'all go on over there and tell her I'll be by directly. Now get."

The two edged toward the door. They knew that to bolt would only bring attention to themselves, and by now they were experts at keeping to the shadows. At the door, they eased out, not letting the rotting wood door slam behind them.

Ramsey turned his attention to the sheriff and the bartender. Cavanaugh was still babbling on. Ramsey listened just long enough to realize that it would take forever for the bartender to get it all out. He wanted to go meet Maybelle, and as soon as possible.

"Maybe I can help clear this up, Sheriff," Ramsey said, moving up alongside the lawman at the bar.

Burleson half turned and looked up at the big Texan. "Oh? And who might you be, boy?"

"Buck Ramsey." He held out his hand, and the sheriff shook it. Ramsey took stock of the lawman in that brief time. Burleson might be a small man, but he carried an air of competence about him. He could, Ramsey figured, fool a lot of people with his looks. They would take him lightly—and then pay a heavy price for it. Ramsey would not.

"So what've you got to tell me, Mr. Ramsey?" he asked in his growly voice.

"Old puss bucket there was bein' a pain in the ass for all concerned. Had half a snootful and was losin' regular at faro. Complainin' about it the whole time, too." Ramsey looked at Cavanaugh. "Gimme me a beer here, would you. And one for the sheriff." He glanced at Burleson. "If you're of a mind?"

"I suppose." He grinned.

When the drinks were served, Ramsey said, "Anyways, two blacks come in here lookin' for me . . ."

"Why?" Burleson interjected.

"Tell me someone was lookin' for me," Ramsey said evenly.

"Who?"

"Don't matter none to this."

Burleson nodded, accepting the rebuff somewhat reluctantly, Ramsey thought.

"Anyway, Cavanaugh was tryin' to find out why they was here, but this damn fool wasn't havin' none of it. Just took it into his mind that he was gonna kill him a couple darkies." Ramsey almost choked on the last word. It was not one he used often, if ever, but he judged it to be necessary considering the circumstances.

Burleson nodded and sipped beer, after removing his cigar momentarily. Foam from the liquid coated his graying, fluffy mustache. "And so you shot him down for givin' a couple darkies a hard time?"

Ramsey looked at him, his eyes hard. Burleson seemed unfazed. "Not quite that simple, Sheriff," Ramsey said. "But it would've been justified even then, considerin' he was stickin' his nose into business didn't concern him."

"So what did happen?"

Ramsey explained it roughly, leaving out some of the nuances, figuring they were not needed.

When Ramsey had finished, Burleson stood leaning against the bar, staring at the Texan. He had his glass in one hand, his cigar stuck in his mouth. He said nothing for some time. Then he offered, "It's a lucky thing for you, Mr. Ramsey, that I know— knew—Clete Skinner so well. He was well-known hereabouts as a bully. He's killed a few men." Burleson smiled wanly. "Mostly ones couldn't protect themselves very well. But he always made it so's it come out self-defense."

Burleson sighed, removed the cigar, sipped beer, and then planted the cigar again. "I knew he'd buy the farm sooner or later, that one day he'd pick on the wrong man. Reckon today was that day and you was that man."

"I reckon," Ramsey said cautiously.

Burleson pulled the cigar out of his mouth once more, and spit out a loose piece of it before sipping some beer. "I'd be obliged, though," he said slowly, "was you not to make a habit of shootin' men down in Dirt Creek, Mr. Ramsey."

"Wasn't plannin' to shoot anybody, Sheriff," Ramsey said. He was a little bothered by the events today. He had never taken lightly to killing.

Burleson nodded. He drained the mug of beer, then planted the cigar back in his mouth. "Obliged for the beer, Mr. Ramsey." He looked at Cavanaugh. "I'll send the undertaker over directly."

He spun and walked out without so much as glancing at the body again.

"You want another beer, Mr. Ramsey?" Cavanaugh asked.

"Nope. Got things to do."

"Well, next time you're in the Red Dog, the drinks'll be on me."

Ramsey looked at the bartender in surprise.

Cavanaugh looked sheepish. "I'm obliged to you, too, Mr. Ramsey," he said softly. It seemed strange coming from so hefty a man as Cavanaugh.

"What for?" Ramsey was still puzzled.

"Well, I was pretty short with them two nigger boys come in here. And for no good reason. If I'd of knowed they was lookin' for you . . ." He paused and coughed in embarrassment. "Anyways, I should've given 'em time to tell why they was in here. They're good boys mostly, Mr. Ramsey. I know that. They don't cause no trouble, don't go where they ain't supposed to. I should've knowed they would've had a good reason for comin' in here like that." He shrugged. "But my mind was elsewhere, I reckon." He sighed. "Anyway, you could've told the sheriff I had given them two boys a hard time and that that's why Skinner jumped in here."

Cavanaugh looked very embarrassed. "And you could've told him that I backed down to Skinner, which brought on a heap of this trouble."

"Wasn't no call to bring all that up," Ramsey said magnanimously, even if it was the truth. Besides, he wasn't about to tell the bartender that he had also done it to keep Douglas and Jackson from being dragged into the mess.

"Well, maybe not," Cavanaugh said doubtfully. "But I'm still obliged. And your drinks are on the house from now on."

"Now I'm obliged to *you*, Mr. Cavanaugh," Ramsey said brightly. "Well, I've got to be goin'. The reason them two boys come in here was to tell me someone was fixin' to meet me."

"Why didn't he just come here and meet you?" Cavanaugh asked, perplexed. "He a parson or something?"

"Wasn't a man, Mr. Cavanaugh," Buck said with a manly wink in the bartender's direction.

"Oh?" Cavanaugh said, wondering. Then he caught on. "Oh! Well, don't let me keep you."

Ramsey strolled outside and stopped. He scanned the street, seeming casual. He saw nothing out of the ordinary—except the undertaker and two helpers hurrying toward the saloon. Ramsey stepped off down the street. Within minutes he was entering the dim confines of Simms's store. He enjoyed most general stores, but this one seemed better than most. It was filled with the smells of leather and coffee and pungent pickles, of sugar and candy and horse grain. It was a jumbled profusion of goods, from ladies' hats to saddles, from longhandles to crackers.

He moved farther into the store, eyes still adjusting to the dimness after the bright sunshine outside. Suddenly he heard a voice at his elbow, "Howdy, Mr. Ramsey."

He turned and looked at Maybelle Sweet. The old woman was about the same as she had been the last time he had seen her. She was stern and formidable-looking despite her sixty-some years but still tall and straight. Her wispy white hair was curled up into a bun, as usual. And she had the old corncob pipe clamped between her still-good teeth.

"Ma'am," Ramsey said. There was real pleasure in his voice.

"You've grown considerable since last time I saw you, boy," Maybelle said. There seemed to be a combination of awe and nonchalance in her voice. She had expected him to grow some more, but she wasn't sure she would have predicted a young man quite this big.

"Yes'm." Ramsey beamed, and he wasn't sure why.

"Took you long enough to get here," Maybelle grumbled.

"Yes'm." Ramsey explained what had transpired.

Maybelle nodded. "I understand, son. But it leaves us short of time."

"For what?"

"Just listen," Maybelle said curtly. "A couple boys from the ranch'll be here directly to take me back." She looked around, making sure no one was near. "Things ain't what they seem over at the Big Horizon."

"I suspected that. I—"

"Hush up." Once more she looked around. "First, I want to tell you that my granddaughter has a powerful hankerin' to see you again, Mr. Ramsey. A *powerful* hankerin'."

Ramsey's heart soared again. He had a thousand questions he wanted to ask, but he knew Maybelle either wouldn't or couldn't answer any of them now.

"No matter what her pa says, she wants to see you again. So I'm invitin' you out to the ranch for supper. Tonight."

"I'll be there," Ramsey vowed. "But what . . ."

"Never you mind," Maybelle said hastily. "Just be there. Six o'clock." She walked away quickly.

Ramsey turned to watch her. She had spotted two cowboys bringing the wagon up to the front of the store. Ramsey figured she didn't want the ranch hands to see her talking to him. So he stayed put until she was on the wagon and heading out of town. With his feet barely touching the ground, Ramsey headed toward his room at the hotel.

CHAPTER

★6★

Ramsey kept it hidden, but he felt some satisfaction at the surprise expressed by Artemis McFarrin when Clarissa, the McFarrin's elderly maid, brought him into the sitting room.

"What're you doing here, Ramsey?" McFarrin asked gruffly.

"Come for supper," Ramsey answered, managing to hide his joy.

"By whose authority?" McFarrin demanded.

"By mine," Maybelle said, sweeping grandly into the room. She laughed a deep, raspy laugh at the discomfit her son-in-law displayed.

"Such a thing ain't right, Mother Maybelle."

Maybelle shrugged. "I invited him, and by cracky, he'll stay."

Ramsey grinned as McFarrin stomped out of the room, muttering. "Ain't you gonna show me around, Mr. McFarrin?" Ramsey asked brightly.

The only response was a growl that fled out of the room on the wind of McFarrin's departure.

Ramsey turned to look at Maybelle. They grinned at each other. "I just love tweakin' that little fool," Maybelle said with another rasping chuckle. "I don't know what Ada June ever saw in him."

Ada June had been the daughter of Maybelle and Caleb Sweet. She had married Artemis McFarrin a little more than twenty years ago. She had given birth to Eula Mae and the twins, Lucius and Edgar. Ada June and Lucius had died on the trip from Texas to the Big Horizon. Ramsey had wondered more than once on that long trek just how someone like Maybelle Sweet could produce a daughter like the sour Ada June McFarrin.

"I often wondered what he saw in her, Miz Maybelle," Ramsey said quietly.

"Me, too," Maybelle chuckled. She was saddened only a little by her daughter's demise. Ada June had been no more of a daughter than she had been a wife—she had done only what propriety called for, and no more.

Ramsey looked perplexed. "Where's Edgar?" he asked. He had wondered all along where the twelve-year-old was but had not had a chance to ask.

Maybelle smiled. "Artemis sent the little pest off to school a way back in Atlanta." She sounded pleased.

Ramsey nodded. He could understand her feeling. The boy always had been something of a troublemaker and prankster.

"Now, Miz Maybelle, if you'd be so kind as to tell me just what's going on around here," he said.

"I would if I . . ." She stopped and turned at the sound of someone entering the room. "Ah, Granddaughter," she said with obvious pleasure. "Come, look at who's here for supper."

"Mr. Ramsey," Eula Mae said demurely.

"Mr. Ramsey, Miss Eula?" Ramsey asked, rather in some surprise. Once again Eula Mae had shown a momentary flash of joy at seeing him. Then it was whisked away, replaced by a frown of . . . of what? Ramsey had no idea.

"Buck," Eula Mae said, ducking her head.

"Well," Maybelle said brightly, "I expect I'll leave you two young people alone—but just to talk, you understand." She buzzed out of the room, shutting the door quietly behind her.

The two stood for a few minutes. Eula Mae looked down at her feet; Ramsey twirled his hat in his hands. There was so much he wanted to say, and to ask, but none of the words would come. Mainly he just wanted to just grab Eula Mae and hold her close.

Eula Mae had the same thoughts going through her head. Still, she refrained from doing or saying anything. Partly it was fear of rejection; partly it was convention. She could not forget that one night, under a wagon, out in the Texas Panhandle. The travelers had holed up in a broken down sod house and fought off the Comanches once. They were waiting for the dawn, when they expected another attack. She had gone to him then. It had been a short, hot night of passion.

Neither of them had ever mentioned it again. Eula Mae was ashamed to, figuring that people would think she was of the lowest sort. Eula Mae thought of herself as chaste most often, but more than once that night had intruded on her consciousness. She usually shivered with the remembrance of that passion and wished she could find it again.

Ramsey also thought of that night with some frequency. It meant more to him than he would let on to anyone, even his brothers. He often thought, though, that he would like to revive what they had managed to find that night. He hoped she was, too. But he was too much of a gentleman to broach the subject. He hadn't had much of a chance to do so anyway, but now here right in front of her, he could not say anything about it.

So they stood, wondering who would make the first move; who would say the first words.

Eula Mae finally decided she would be the first. After all, she thought, she had been the one who had left Ramsey, choosing to go off with her father. It was the right thing, she had thought then. Now she was not so sure. She had thought frequently in the past three years that what she should have done was to tell her father to hire a maid and gone off with Ramsey.

It was too late for that now, but she could try to make sure she did not waste any more of their time apart. There was, of course, a problem that would have to be resolved, but she would worry about that later.

Her head came up slowly, and she flashed a small, uncertain smile at him. She was encouraged when he returned it. Eula Mae moved forward slowly, gaining confidence with each step.

The next thing she knew, she was in Ramsey's strong embrace, and her head was against his broad chest. She was comforted by the strength she felt there. After a bit, she tilted her head back to look up at him. "I'm glad you came, Buck," she said softly. She waited to be kissed.

Ramsey looked down at the pale face with the long eyelashes framing the bright blue eyes. He wondered how he could have stayed away from her for three years. He had become something of a womanizer in that time, but he realized now that none of those others meant anything. He had to admit, that most of those others were fallen women, but there had been a few good ones along the way. Ones like Grace Red Bird, the beautiful Cherokee who had captured his heart for a short spell. But none could compare with the golden haired beauty in his arms. He obliged by planting a powerful strong kiss on her willing, generous mouth.

"Now," Ramsey said after they had broken a little apart, "what's going on around here?"

"What do you mean?" Eula Mae countered, batting her long lashes innocently at him.

"Something ain't right around here . . ."

"Seemed just fine to me," Eula Mae offered with a giggle.

"Damnit, Eula, you know what I mean." The kiss and his thoughts had left his blood boiling, and it made him rather short-tempered.

"No, I don't," Eula Mae said guilelessly.

Ramsey paced a little. "I can feel in my bones that something's wrong. And I want to know what it is," he insisted.

"Nothing's wrong," Eula Mae said. She began to close up to him. She had always been stubborn; she had not changed.

"Damnit, Eula," Ramsey snapped, swinging around to face her. "I can help. Whatever it is."

Eula Mae nodded. It was the second reason she was glad he had come back. She wanted his help. She smiled at him. "It's . . ."

Eula Mae stopped when there was a knock at the door, followed by Maybelle's irritated voice, "We have visitors, Eula Mae."

"Who would be . . ." Ramsey asked softly, looking in surprise at Eula Mae.

She held a finger to his lips. A serious, haunted look had come over her. "Just keep quiet. Please."

Ramsey nodded once, befuddled but not showing it.

"Come in, Granny," Eula Mae called. Her face seemed composed now, though Ramsey could tell from the stiff set of her back that she was disturbed by something.

The door opened and Maybelle entered, followed by a tall, elegantly dressed man a few years older than Ramsey. He had an arrogant cast to his face, and gave off an aura of money and special circumstance.

The man stopped just inside the door, his look of expectancy giving way to one of annoyance. "Who the hell is this?" he asked.

Ramsey was amazed; it seemed that the man's voice, rather than his bloodless lips, had sneered.

"Watch your tongue, son," Maybelle said. "There's ladies about."

"One anyway," the man said. He looked balefully at Maybelle, as if daring her to challenge him.

She released her raspy laugh, annoying and perplexing the newcomer.

"Who is this man?" he asked, seeming to strive for at least a modicum of politeness.

"Colin," Eula Mae said, "I'd like you to meet an old friend, Buck Ramsey. Buck, Colin Weymouth."

Ramsey slapped his hat on and held out his hand. Weymouth ignored it, preferring to stare at him like he was a bird looking over a particularly juicy worm.

Ramsey's eyes narrowed as he dropped his hand. Anger bubbled up into his throat, but he contained it, with an effort.

"Who is he?" Weymouth asked, the arrogance soaring through the words.

"Like I said, an old friend," Eula Mae said tightly.

It was plain to Ramsey that she was afraid of Colin Weymouth, and he wondered why. He also suspected that Weymouth was somehow a major part of whatever was wrong at the Big Horizon Ranch.

"What's he doing here?" Weymouth's English accent was very evident.

"I invited him to sup with us," Maybelle said. The old woman had no fear of this young man. He could do nothing to her.

"I don't like it," Weymouth said, as if that would be the end of it.

"Too bad," Maybelle said. "He's an old family friend. Did us many a favor back some time ago. He's been invited, and he's stayin'."

"Someday you'll go too far, you old hag."

Maybelle grinned up at him, daring him to do something. She was too old to worry about fear and pain and death. She also wanted to see him do something in front of Buck Ramsey. The young Texan was far more of a gentleman than this cultured, fancy-pants Englishman ever would be. At the same time, Ramsey was far tougher.

Ramsey was shocked that a man who considered himself a gentleman would speak to an old woman in such a manner. He was on the verge of smashing Weymouth's face, but Eula Mae's hand on his arm stayed him. He settled for filing the information away. He would not forget it, and he vowed that one day Mr. Colin Weymouth would be made to pay for the insulting remark, and for his smugness.

Clarissa popped her white-haired head in the door and said, "Supper be served."

The four people in the room remained standing in a dragging silence. Finally Eula Mae wrapped a hand around Ramsey's arm and they walked out, moving past a suddenly livid Colin

Weymouth. The Englishman followed stiffly behind them, with Maybelle the last out.

Ramsey felt uncomfortable with Weymouth behind him, but the walk to the dining room was mercifully brief. The dinner was not. There was a heavy silence in the air, though Maybelle eventually managed to lighten it a little with some stories of the old days. Ramsey even began to enjoy himself a little.

After the meal, the men retired to McFarrin's den. McFarrin passed around cigars, which Ramsey refused, and glasses of good bourbon, which Ramsey did not refuse.

Once they were all seated, Weymouth asked gruffly, "What're you doing here, Mr. . . . was it Ramsey?"

"Ramsey, yes."

"What're you doing here?"

"Havin' an after-supper snort of bourbon," Ramsey said blandly.

McFarrin almost smiled, while Weymouth choked on his whiskey. "Very humorous, Mr. Ramsey," Weymouth finally allowed. "Now answer my question." It was a command.

"I did." Ramsey matched the Englishman's stare.

Weymouth took some time in controlling himself. When he did, he went on calmly. "Perhaps you do not understand, Mr. Ramsey." The voice was smooth, glib. "I am courting Miss Eula. I have been for some months, and I believe she is near to pledging her troth to me."

"So?" Ramsey's back was up now, and he would go out of his way to irritate this pompous Englishman.

"So," Weymouth said, seething, "you have been warned."

"Warned about what?" Ramsey asked in mock innocence.

"Damn your eyes," Weymouth snapped. Once more he made an effort to control his emotions. "Let me make it perfectly clear to you, Mr. Ramsey. Miss Eula is mine."

Out of the corner of his eye, Ramsey saw McFarrin start. Anger flickered in McFarrin's eyes, but he said nothing.

"We'll just see about that, Mr. Weymouth," Ramsey said evenly.

"There is nothing to see about, Mr. Ramsey," Weymouth hissed. "I have explained the situation. Miss Eula is mine. I will brook no interference in my pursuit of her."

"Don't make me no never mind what you will or won't brook, Weymouth. Until Miss Eula herself tells me to hit the trail, I aim to hang around some." Ramsey finished his drink and stood. There was no question that he was vowing to challenge Weymouth for the love of Miss Eula Mae McFarrin.

Ramsey set his glass down on the table. "Now, sir, I expect you—and I—have worn out our welcome here for one night."

"Shit," Weymouth snorted. "I'll stay here as long as I damn well please."

"You'll leave now," Ramsey said simply.

Weymouth was about to retort, but something stayed the words. He looked up at this big, hard-muscled young man and began to think that perhaps he should leave. He downed the rest of his drink and stood. "It is getting late," he said lamely. Without another word, he headed out.

Ramsey followed more slowly. Eula Mae waved goodbye to him just before he went though the front door.

CHAPTER

★ 7 ★

Ramsey spent as much time out at the ranch as he thought he could get away with. It wasn't much, and he and Eula Mae never had any time to be alone. Artemis McFarrin had voiced some displeasure at Ramsey's visits several times.

Finally Ramsey had looked him square in the eye and said, "I'm in love with your daughter, Mr. McFarrin. And I aim to make her mine someday—if she'll have me."

"I ain't so sure I approve, Buck," McFarrin said with a frown.

"You won't have no say in it," Ramsey snapped. Then he sighed. "We've had our differences, Mr. McFarrin, but I thought we were over all that. Maybe not. Still, I'm here, and I aim to stay." He scratched the stubble on his face. "And I'd like to help you with whatever is plaguin' you folks."

McFarrin shrugged, unconvinced, but Ramsey suspected that McFarrin was afraid or worried. Maybe both.

Ramsey was perplexed about that, as well as about what was going on at the Big Horizon. He also was frustrated at not being able to learn anything, and thus do anything to help the McFarrins.

The visits did serve to annoy Colin Weymouth, though, and that gave Ramsey more than a little pleasure.

When he was not at the ranch, Ramsey poked around in Dirt Creek, seeking to find out anything he could about Colin Weymouth and the Big Horizon. Information was scarce, and people seemed afraid to talk. In frustration, he quit asking questions and instead just kept his eyes and ears open as he hung around the three saloons and two brothels in town, as well as anywhere else he might find people talking.

It took more than three days, but he finally managed to piece together a little information. He learned that the Englishman—something obvious from his accent—was the son of some minor nobleman and had come to Colorado Territory straight from England. From what Ramsey could learn, he deduced that although Weymouth's father was only a minor nobleman, he was blessed with considerable wealth.

That baffled him all the more. After he learned that, he sat in the Red Dog Saloon, sipping a beer, thinking about it. He couldn't help but wonder what the son of a rich English nobleman was doing in some backwater place like Dirt Creek. Ramsey had heard that quite a few Englishmen with money to burn were forming corporations and buying up ranches in the United States. There was, Ramsey figured, a chance that that was what Weymouth was doing here.

Still, that didn't make much sense. He could find no evidence that Weymouth was involved in such a thing. He also figured that if he was as rich as word had it, then Weymouth would have his pick of ranches across the West. He would not have to focus on the Big Horizon.

Unless, of course, Miss Eula Mae McFarrin was the Englishman's real focus. Ramsey didn't like that possibility; he didn't even like to think about it. He realized, however, that such a possibility was highly likely, and, from Weymouth's standpoint highly desirable. In such a case, not only would Weymouth win himself possibly the most beautiful and sought after woman in all the territory, he also would be able to lay claim to the Big Horizon Ranch one day without having to put out any cash for it.

As much as he hated to think about such a thing, Ramsey had to acknowledge that it made sense, though how and why Weymouth had gravitated to such a remote place as Dirt Creek still perplexed him. He could understand how, once Weymouth got here and saw Eula Mae that he might hang around. But why come here in the first place? That was one of the important questions for which Ramsey could find no answer.

He was immersed in such thoughts when Sheriff Burleson arrived and plunked himself into a chair across the table from Ramsey. The Texan shook himself from his brooding thoughts and acknowledged the lawman's presence with a nod. "What can I do for you, Sheriff?" he asked politely. He was, however, rather annoyed at the intrusion.

"Get me a beer for starters," Burleson allowed with a short smile.

Ramsey, who was still drinking on the gratitude of Cavanaugh, ordered the beer. Burleson pulled the cigar out of his mouth, took a long sip, and stuck the cigar back into his foam-coated mustache.

"I hear you been spendin' a heap of time out at the Big Horizon, Mr. Ramsey," Burleson said with little inflection.

"Some." Ramsey was wary. This should be none of the lawman's business.

"Some folks don't take kindly to that."

"What folks?" Ramsey thought he knew.

"Interested folks," Burleson said tightly.

"Was it Miss Eula? Or her pa?"

"Not directly." Burleson seemed a little uncomfortable.

"Colin Weymouth?" Ramsey asked sharply.

The sheriff went through the ritual with the cigar and the beer. He said nothing, but his face told Ramsey that he had been right all along. When Burleson was finished with the maneuver, he said, "I think y'all ought to spend a heap less time out there, Mr. Ramsey."

"So Weymouth has a clear shot at Miss Eula?" Ramsey asked, feigning disbelief. "You got to be joshin' me, Sheriff."

"I'm serious."

"Until Miss Eula tells me herself to stay away, I aim to go out to the ranch every chance I get." The words were harsh, and Ramsey's eyes reflected the depths of his determination.

"It'll be the cause of a heap of trouble, boy," Burleson said. He sort of admired this hard young man. But he knew there was no bucking wealth and position. He had learned that long ago, and knew it to be a truism that never failed.

"I've seen trouble before."

"I suspect you have." Burleson went through the action with the cigar and beer, draining his mug. He stuffed the cigar into his face and stood. "Well, Mr. Ramsey, you've been issued your warnin'. I can't help you none should you choose to pay it no heed."

"Just don't get in my way, Sheriff," Ramsey said coldly, "and we'll have no trouble."

Burleson glared at him a moment. He was unafraid—he had seen gun punks by the dozens in his forty-two years, and had tamed more than his share of them. But once again he felt a twinge of admiration for Ramsey, and he would sort of hate to see the young man come to a bad end. "I'll do whatever is my duty, son," he said before turning and strolling casually away.

So, Ramsey thought, *Weymouth's got the sheriff in his pocket.* That could create problems, but Ramsey decided it was not worth worrying about. What bothered him more was the sheriff's attitude, and the fact that he was doing Weymouth's bidding. Money could make a big difference in a man's life. Ramsey had none, and had little prospects of ever accumulating any.

Buck Ramsey was a prideful man, as were all the Ramseys. But it was not an arrogant pride, just the pride of being a Ramsey, a man with a family that was close no matter how far and wide the members might be scattered. He had always taken pride in being what he was—an honest, hard-working, truthful man. He gave others their due, when they earned it, and always treated women with the utmost respect.

He had realized the other day, when he had gone to the Big Horizon for the first time, that he loved Miss Eula Mae McFarrin. He was fairly—no, very—certain that she returned that feeling. He began to wonder now, though, if perhaps he was being unfair to her. How could he expect their love to grow when he had so little to offer her?

Weymouth could give Eula Mae everything that Ramsey could not—money, position, even a title someday, Ramsey supposed. Weymouth was a handsome enough man, Ramsey admitted to himself, tall and well-built. Only his arrogance and the condescension spawned by too much money were drawbacks.

What can I give her? Ramsey wondered. He allowed as that he might be handsome enough. He would certainly work hard enough to make the ranch pay. Still, it was small potatoes compared with what Weymouth could offer her.

Ramsey was almost convinced that he would leave off courting Eula Mae, that he would try to help the McFarrins and then ride out. It might hurt Eula Mae a little—he hoped it would, anyway—but he figured she would get over it soon enough. Especially when she married Weymouth. As for him, well, he figured he would carry the hurt with him for the rest of his days.

Then he just as quickly decided that all those gloomy thoughts were so much rubbish. He might be a prideful man, and a mostly common one, but he was also as stubborn and as mule-headed as any man alive. He would not be forced to walk away from the woman he loved and desired above all others. Not by some fancy-pants Englishman. He smiled to himself and saluted his decision with a goodly swallow of beer.

To celebrate, he wandered over to the hovel of a brothel and picked out a woman who had satirically chosen the name Chastity. She was about the fairest-looking woman in the brood, though that was not saying much. She was short and far too skinny, what with her ribs sticking out all over. She had a pinched, creased face. Her hands were rough-skinned and none too gentle in their touch. She was a mighty poor substitute for Eula Mae, but she was better than anything else he would find in town, Ramsey figured.

Feeling somewhat sated, Ramsey headed out afterward over to the Red Dog. After a beer, he went back to his room and cleaned up. Then he saddled Biscuit and rode out to the ranch. He stuck to the shadows, not going straight to the house. He rode over the swelling land, watching the lowing cows grazing placidly on the lush summer grass. He followed a creek for a bit, until it came to a large pond fed by a spring. It was a pleasant place, shaded by Osage orange, ash, and cottonwood trees as well as chokecherries, hackberries, and other brush. It was cool in the shade, and the bubbling spring and creek were soothing.

As Ramsey let the ginger-colored horse drink, he took a look around. The place was out of the way, but not hidden except by two very small humps of land, really nothing more than gentle swells. He wondered why McFarrin had not built the ranch house close to this spot, but then decided it was that McFarrin was a smart enough rancher to know that such a special place would quickly become fouled by the presence of people.

Ramsey mounted up and rode on off, meandering across the vast acreage of the Big Horizon. He didn't know what he was looking for, or even if he was looking for anything. He just wanted a chance to see the ranch, and to let his eyes wander. He had found that by doing that, sometimes answers popped up right in front of his face.

Such was not to be the case this time, and after two hours of aimless and fruitless wandering, he turned his horse for the house.

He and Eula Mae had time for only one quick, stolen kiss before Artemis McFarrin was there and halfheartedly welcoming him. Fifteen minutes later, Weymouth showed up, looking sour when he caught sight of Ramsey. The Texan grinned insolently at the Englishman.

"Have you spoken with the sheriff lately, Mr. Ramsey?" Weymouth asked in the few moments the two men had alone in the den. McFarrin had gone out of the room to see about dinner. He half hoped that his daughter's two beaus would settle their differences while he was gone.

"Yep," Ramsey said with a small, ingratiating smile.

"And?" Weymouth asked, letting some of his exasperation show.

Ramsey looked around to make sure none of the women were around. "And I told him he was pokin' the wrong cow," he said blandly.

Weymouth looked confused. By the time the meaning of the statement began to sink in, his face flushed with anger. He was about to retort when McFarrin's return made him clamp his lips together. He seethed, and his eyes bored hot holes into Ramsey.

The Texan smiled like he had not a care in the world. Which, he realized, was pretty much the case.

Supper was once again a strained affair. Even Maybelle's chatter did little to lighten the mood. It was almost with relief that Ramsey left, making sure that Weymouth was heading out, too. Ramsey rode swiftly down the trail, past the sign to the ranch and then cut off and rode cross-country until he was behind a low ridge. He ground-staked Biscuit and walked to the top of the ridge. He sat and watched.

The full moon shed plenty of light, so he could see Weymouth's buggy coming down the lane. He, too, veered off just after passing the sign. He pulled the buggy around in a wide circle and back onto the road.

It was all Ramsey needed to see. He ran down the hill, leaped on Biscuit, and galloped around the other side of the hill. He was sitting in the middle of the road to the ranch house, his Winchester across the saddle in front of him, when Weymouth came clattering up.

Weymouth's face was almost comical in its rage when he spotted Ramsey, who said politely, "You're headin' the wrong way, Weymouth."

"What business is it of yours, Ramsey?" Weymouth hissed.

"Where it concerns Miss Eula—and the rest of the McFarrin family—everything concerns me." He leaned forward, resting his arms on the saddlehorn. "Now, I don't know what the hell your game is, Weymouth," Ramsey said harshly. "But I figure it bodes ill for the McFarrins."

"How dare you speak to me in such a way," Weymouth spat. He was indignant.

"I'll talk to you any goddamn way I please," Ramsey said easily. "And," he added, straightening, "I aim to keep my eyes on you, boy. You make one stupid move, and I'll plant your ass in the boneyard without a thought."

Weymouth controlled himself only with a great effort. "Do you know who you're dealing with, you backwoods ruffian?"

"Yep—a no-'count dandy of a peckerwood," Ramsey snarled. "Now, haul that wagon round and head on home."

"And you?" Weymouth asked. He had brought himself under control. He knew he could not take this man down here and now; it was evident that Ramsey was well-versed in the Colt's pistol he wore at his hip, and in the Winchester repeating rifle lying across the saddle. Weymouth decided he would find a more fitting way to get Mr. Buck Ramsey.

"I'll be followin' you to make sure you don't have another change of heart—or direction."

CHAPTER

★ 8 ★

Maybelle sent word to Ramsey the next day that it might be better if he did not come for supper that night. Her note also said that she had made the same request of Weymouth and that if he showed up, she would turn him away.

Ramsey was some disappointed in that, but he figured there was no harm done. He would miss seeing Eula Mae, of course, and even Maybelle. Other than that, he saw no real problem with it. Still, old Clarissa's cooking was far superior to the swill usually served up in the dining room of Wohlford's Hostelry and Chop House. That was nothing to look forward to.

Before supper, Ramsey fortified himself with two mugs of beer and a shot of good bourbon. Then he strolled into the dining room of the hotel and ordered up. The only good thing he found about it was the peach cobbler he had after finishing his stringy beefsteak and mushy potatoes.

To keep his mind off the food, he thought about Eula Mae, and, of course, Weymouth. Whenever he thought of Eula Mae these days, Weymouth intruded. Something would have to be done soon about the Englishman, he knew. What he didn't know, was what.

Weymouth had been beside himself with anger the night before as Ramsey rode warily behind the Englishman's buggy almost the full way to Weymouth's house. Weymouth had one of the very few houses sitting just outside town, up on the flat ridges. It served to show everyone that he was above the common folk. It was another irritant to Ramsey.

Weymouth did not know it, but Ramsey waited around in the shadows of a building just off the track leading to Weymouth's

46

house. After an hour, Ramsey figured that Weymouth was at home for the night, especially when several horses and buggies rode up that way and parked and their passengers strolled into the house.

Ramsey suspected that he ought to just up and shoot Weymouth. He could do it on a dark night with no one around. There would be no one to prove he was in any way connected with it. Ramsey was sure that would solve the problem once and for all.

However, Ramsey knew there were problems involved in that. For one thing, Weymouth had really done nothing wrong. He had only threatened Ramsey over the affections of Eula Mae. That was certainly understandable. Besides, Ramsey suspected that Weymouth was involved in far more than just courting Eula Mae, something far deeper and possibly destructive for Artemis McFarrin and his family. Ramsey wanted to find out first if that was true and, if it was, what it was. Then he thought he could act freely—and as harshly as the situation demanded.

With the less-than-splendid supper sitting like a soggy log in his stomach, Ramsey wandered outside. He stopped to take in the fresh, warm air. It was a pleasant night. The hint of a breeze brought the smells of the town softly to him; the temperature was just about right. There had been no rain in several days, and the sky indicated there would be none for several more. Ramsey did not mind. Rain would make the trip out to the Big Horizon all the longer, as the road would turn into thick, soupy mud.

Ramsey burped, and then winced at the unpleasant reminder of his dinner. It tended to sour some the pleasurable feelings the night had given him.

With a sigh, Ramsey stepped off the boardwalk and into the street. Not only was the hotel one of the few wood buildings in town, it also was one of the few with a sidewalk. A rangy mongrel trotted over and began sniffing at Ramsey's leg. "Get, dog," Ramsey growled softly.

The dog paid him no heed, so Ramsey launched a boot at the animal. It wasn't much of a kick, but Ramsey just wanted to discourage the mongrel, not hurt it. The cur yelped in surprise and backed off.

"Go on home, you dumb dog," Ramsey said good-naturedly.

The dog wandered off, sniffing like crazy. Ramsey felt a smile creep over his face at the animal's antics. He strode off, heading for the Red Dog. He stopped for a moment, half turning, thinking there was something he needed from his room at the hotel.

He fell when he felt a fiery sizzling across his chest. As he was going down, he heard the report of a gun. He dropped his Winchester in the fall, and he sucked in his breath when he hit, both from the impact of the fall and the hot pain that burned across his lower chest.

"Goddamn," he muttered. He started to push himself up, when another bullet kicked up a clod of earth next to him. He flopped back down, partly on his left side and partly on his back. He decided in that instant after the second bullet that he had better play possum. He knew he would be dead soon if he didn't do something.

As he lay there waiting for his attacker to show himself, Ramsey sweated. He hoped the man wouldn't just put another bullet into him while he was lying there and then go off without ever showing himself. Ramsey prayed that the man would want to make sure of his handiwork. Ramsey would do so in such a case, mainly because it was so dark, and one could never be sure at night if the shot was fatal.

He also moved his hand up very slowly and eased out the Colt pistol. He thumbed back the hammer, holding the pistol at arm's length down his leg. He waited, trying not to think of the burning pain in his chest. He wondered if he was mortally wounded, but he seemed to be too strong for that.

The wait seemed interminable to him but in reality was little more than a minute. He heard footsteps in the dirt. And voices:

"Best hurry it up and get this over with, Vince," one voice said.

"Yep," another added. "The law'll be here soon."

"I know that," a third voice responded. "But I want to make sure the bastard's dead. I don't like leavin' a job unfinished."

"Looks dead to me," the first voice said.

"Could be fakin', Carl. You ought to know that."

"You're just a worry-wart, Vince," a man said with a low chuckle. Neither of the other two joined in, and the chuckles faded rapidly into the night.

With his peripheral vision, Ramsey saw three pairs of legs amble into his view. He knew he could not wait any longer. He had to move. Taking three men out with a pistol was going to be no mean feat even under the best of circumstances. In the dark, and being wounded, he wasn't sure of the results at all.

Ramsey jerked upward, using his stomach muscles. He ignored the searing pain that ripped across his chest, as he came to rest, sitting legs bent out in front of him, the pistol at arm's length.

"Shoot me, will you, you sons a bitches," he snarled as he fired.

Unconsciously, he had gone for the man named Vince first. He didn't know how he knew who Vince was, nor was he sure that Vince was the leader of these three. But the others had treated him as the leader, and Ramsey instinctively picked him out.

Vince went down without a sound, two bullets in his narrow chest. His finger twitched involuntarily, firing off the Winchester rifle he carried barrel downward in his right hand. The bullet buried itself in the dirt.

Ramsey did not see Vince fall. He swung his pistol toward another target and continued to fire.

"Jesus Christ," the one named Carl bellowed at the first shot. He jerked his own pistol up, but dropped it when one of Ramsey's bullets broke the bone in his upper arm.

In alarm, Ramsey fired twice more at Carl. He knew that would leave him with an empty pistol, but he had to make sure. It was with a bit of relief that he saw the third assailant turn and race off into the night, almost knocking down several men who had come out of the saloon at the sound of the gunshots.

The last two bullets Ramsey fired both hit Carl, one in the leg, the other just above the mouth. Carl slumped in a bloody heap in the dirt. He lay there, moaning.

Ramsey rolled to his side, so he was on his hands and knees. He pushed himself up awkwardly, trying not to exacerbate the pain in his chest. He dropped his Colt into his holster. Spotting his Winchester, he stumbled to it and picked it up. He angrily levered a round into the chamber and looked around, glaring at any and all who had come to see what the commotion was all about.

Ramsey felt the rising tide of rage welling up inside him. He was furious that someone would try to kill him, for no apparent reason. Making it worse was that it had happened under the cover of night. To Buck Ramsey, that was not very honorable.

Sheriff Woody Burleson ran up, pistol out. He stopped several feet from Ramsey, glanced at the bodies and then at Ramsey holding the rifle.

"Drop the rifle, Ramsey," Burleson said quietly.

"Put your pistol away first," Ramsey snarled. He had been shot at enough for one night, he figured. If Burleson wanted to shoot at him, the lawman would have to pay for it in blood.

Burleson glared at him a moment. Then he nodded. He uncocked his pistol, dropped it in the holster, and even slid the small loop over the hammer.

Ramsey nodded in return. He uncocked the Winchester and rested it in the crook of his left arm.

"Want to tell me what happened, Buck?"

"These fellers took a couple shots at me. Damned near killed me. I figured I needed to discourage them from tryin' again."

"Damn, Ramsey, I told you I didn't want this kind of crap going on in Dirt Creek."

"I didn't start it, Sheriff," Ramsey reminded him in none too polite tones.

"Dirt Creek used to be a peaceable town, Ramsey. Till you showed up."

"That's a load of steer shit, and you damn well know it," Ramsey spit.

"Maybe, kid. But trouble seems to follow you around like a calf its mother. I ain't of a mind to put up with such things in my town. Now . . ."

Ramsey leaned back against the corner of a building and sighed, trying to cool the fires of pain in his chest.

"You hurt, boy?" Burleson asked. He was surprised that he had not thought to check before.

"Some." Ramsey had been afraid to look down and see what the damage actually was. He knew his shirt was blood-soaked and that his chest hurt like all hell fire. That was all he needed to know for now.

Burleson moved up close to him. In the darkness, he had not been able to see the dark blood on Ramsey's shirt. Now he took it in. He parted the shirt as gently as he could and took a glance underneath. "Don't seem fatal," he said, stepping back a little. "But I expect it'll need a doctor's care."

Ramsey nodded. "If you're done askin' questions, I'll see to it."

"They got you first?" Burleson asked softly. He was fairly certain he knew.

"Yep. I was walkin' along mindin' my own business. Next thing I know, I'm laying in the dirt, chest bleedin'."

"Where'd it come from?"

"No idea. I suspect, now that I think about it, that they were standin' over alongside Spillman's Bakery."

"Just the two of 'em?"

"Nope. There was a third. He took off a-runnin' when I started shootin' back."

"Any idea of who was behind this?"

"Nope," Ramsey said blandly. Both he and Burleson had their suspicions. It could have been only one man would concoct such a thing here in Dirt Creek. No one else in town really knew Ramsey all that well. The only other possibility was that it was some long-lost relative of Clete Skinner come for revenge. But that was unlikely.

"All right," Burleson said, jerking his head, "go on and see the doc. I'll mosey on by tomorrow if I got anything else to ask."

"I can't wait," Ramsey responded sarcastically. He headed off in the direction of the doctor's office.

Burleson did drop by the next day, but Ramsey thought it was more to see how he was doing than to ask questions about last night's events. The wound was not as bad as Ramsey had feared—just a shallow trench at a slight angle across the area where abdomen and chest met. It still hurt like hell, but otherwise it was not very debilitating.

It did not stop him from riding out to the Big Horizon that night; nor did it stop him from enjoying the sympathy expressed by Eula Mae and her grandmother. Weymouth sat through it all with a stern, sour look on his flat face.

The two competitors for Eula Mae's hand left together again, and outside, Ramsey said, "Think I'll escort you home, Mr. Weymouth." There was just a hint of steel in his words and voice. "Make sure nothin' happens to you."

Weymouth was torn between rage and fear. He more than half suspected that Ramsey figured he was behind the assault last night. He also was fairly certain that Ramsey was planning to kill him on the trail.

Ramsey knew the thoughts going through Weymouth's mind, and he did nothing to ease the Englishman's fear. He figured it best to let Weymouth stew. He said nothing on the trip; he just rode along watchfully.

At they reached the track toward Weymouth's home, Ramsey said, "Don't send no more guns after me, Weymouth." Then he turned the horse and galloped into town.

CHAPTER

★ 9 ★

Within a couple of days, Ramsey was pretty well recovered. He felt considerable relief in knowing that he would not undergo a sharp, lancing pain every time he took a deep breath.

He had gone out to the Big Horizon each night for supper. With Weymouth also there, they were not very pleasant experiences, but Ramsey felt he had to go. For one thing, just being in Eula Mae's presence was a blessing to him. For another, he could not give Weymouth any advantage whatsoever in his pursuit of Eula Mae. He had to keep an eye on the Englishman for that reason, and to try to see that Weymouth hired no more men to gun him down.

Then one night Weymouth tried to win Eula's Mae's favors with bluster and his usual arrogance. When Eula Mae was having none of that, he turned sullen. He stayed that way for the next couple of nights.

Though Ramsey never really got any time alone with Eula Mae, he felt the tide of her favor turning in his direction. He felt sure she would say goodbye to Colin Weymouth sooner or later and take up with him again. He also had become certain that whatever was bothering Eula Mae and her family was somehow connected with Weymouth. He was concerned that the situation would have to be cleared up before Eula Mae would—or could—get rid of Weymouth.

What irritated Ramsey so much was that he was basically helpless. He wanted to help the McFarrins. Not only because of Eula Mae, but also because he liked Maybelle and even Artemis. But mostly it was because of Eula Mae. If he could fix whatever was wrong here, he felt certain that she would banish Weymouth from the Big Horizon. Ramsey looked forward to that day, but wondered if he would ever be able to do anything to hasten its arrival.

It occupied his mind almost all the time these days, but that did not keep him from being alert. It was something he assumed he had inherited from Matt and Kyle. Both older brothers were that way. They could have a thousand things on their minds at any one time, but they were always alert to danger. His other brothers, Amos, the oldest of all the Ramseys, and Luke, who was just a little older than Buck, did not possess such a facility. Buck had often wondered if he, Matt, and Kyle had acquired that talent because of the life they lived, or if they lived that life because they had the trait. There was no answer, he had long ago reasoned.

That ability seemed heightened these days, since the three gunmen had attacked him. He had not learned anything about the men. No one in Dirt Creek seemed to know them or when they had arrived in town. They were as much a mystery as everything else that surrounded Ramsey.

Still, Ramsey did keep on his toes as he wandered around Dirt Creek or rode through the grasslands of the Big Horizon.

Four days after being wounded, he was walking down the main street of Dirt Creek, heading for the Red Dog. He was bored, and his wound itched as it healed, making him irritable. Always alert, he watched as a small carriage pulled to a stop just ahead of him. There was nothing outstanding about the carriage. It was one of the occupants that had caught his attention.

The young woman was nearly the equal of Eula Mae in beauty. She had pale, almost white hair, which framed a delicately boned face that was surprisingly soft looking despite the prominent cheek-and chin bones. She sat on the carriage seat with grace and dignity, her small hands demurely folded in her lap. Her clothes were of the best materials and workmanship. Her bonnet and draw-string purse matched the brightly flowered dress.

As Ramsey neared the carriage, the young woman started to alight, not bothering to wait for the older man next to her to help. Her foot slipped on the carriage step and she started to tumble.

Ramsey was right there at the time. He dropped the Winchester and instinctively reached out and grabbed her, preventing her from crashing to the ground.

She was as light as a feather and much tinier than Ramsey had expected, and he had no trouble lifting her under the arms and setting her down gently on her feet. He kept his hands on her a moment, wanting to make sure she had gotten her bearings.

"You all right, miss?" he asked.

"Oh, yes, sir," she said. She batted her lashes and fanned herself with a hand. "I might've been hurt something awful, if you . . ."

"Unhand my daughter, you scoundrel," a voice thundered.

Ramsey looked over at the man who had been in the carriage with the woman. He was now standing next to the girl, a flabby arm protectively around her shoulders.

"You talkin' to me?" Ramsey asked, glaring angrily at the man. Any joy he might have felt at seeing this beautiful young woman and from helping her was fading quickly.

"I was," the man said. He sounded offended, indignant.

Ramsey released the girl and turned to face the man. "You ought to learn what you're talkin' about before you go spoutin' off, mister," he said mostly calmly. "If it wasn't for me, your daughter'd be lying in a heap on the ground now."

"Don't insult me, young man," the man intoned. His bushy white eyebrows had a movement all their own, jerking up and down, though the rest of the man's face was unmoving.

"I ain't insulted you, mister," Ramsey said in warning. "Yet."

"You villainous upstart," the man bellowed. "Sheriff! Where's the sheriff? Good Lord, a woman can't even set foot upon the streets of Dirt Creek anymore without being accosted by thugs. What's this town coming to?"

He glanced around, anger growing. "Sheriff? Where is that useless lawman? Where is he?"

"Right here, Ardmore," Burleson said as he pushed his way through the crowd that had gathered. "Now, what're you roaring about?"

"Arrest that man," Ardmore said sharply. He pointed at Ramsey.

"For what?" Burleson asked. He was impatient, but not sure at what.

"For taking indecent liberties with my daughter." He fairly shook with outraged indignation. "Right here on the streets. In broad daylight. The shame. The shame of it."

"That right, Miss Helen?"

"Well," Helen said coyly, drawing the word out. She seemed reluctant to talk.

"Well, did he or didn't he?" Burleson asked in some exasperation.

Ramsey straightened from having picked up his Winchester. "All I did was catch her as she stumbled getting out of the coach," he said evenly. He was trying to keep the heat of his anger under wraps, at least for the time being.

"I want to hear what she has to say, Ramsey," Burleson snapped. "Well, Miss Helen?"

Helen coughed delicately. "It's true that I stumbled getting out of the carriage," she said. "And it's true that he caught me." She flushed in embarrassment. "But, well . . ."

"Out with it, girl," Burleson snapped. The situation was getting ridiculous, he thought. He wanted to get this cleared up and head off to his midday meal.

"She should not have to answer such questions out here in front of all these others," Ardmore said. He sounded offended.

Burleson shrugged. "Answer me, girl. Or you and your pa can go about your business and leave me to mine."

"It is a delicate subject, Sheriff," Helen said, looking shyly at the lawman. "A lady doesn't usually mention such things in mixed company."

"I understand, miss," Burleson said. He removed his hat and scratched the growing bald spot at the crown of his head. "But this is not a usual time. And unless you tell me there's some reason to arrest Mr. Ramsey, I'm going to let him go."

"Well," Helen started again. She looked at Ramsey almost apologetically. "He did save me from falling, and for that I'm grateful." She paused, took a deep breath and then plunged ahead. "But it does seem he left his hands on me somewhat longer than a gentleman should." The voice faded near the end as she hid her head in shame.

"You happy now, Sheriff?" Ardmore growled. He pulled his daughter a little closer, trying to shield her from prying eyes. "Now arrest that scoundrel and lock him up."

"Let's go, Ramsey," Burleson said with finality. "Hand over the Winchester, and the Colt and march on up to the jail."

Ramsey stood there looking at the lawman coldly. He was dangling on the verge of action. In two seconds, he figured, he could shoot down the sheriff and Ardmore. The confusion that followed would allow him to escape.

"Now, Ramsey!" Burleson snapped. He was edgy. He had enough sense to know he could not take Ramsey in a fair fight, either with fist or gun. And he did not want any trouble here.

Ramsey decided. He handed the rifle over, butt first. With two fingers, he pulled the Colt out of the holster and handed that to the sheriff, too.

Burleson breathed in relief. "All right, Buck, let's go."

Ramsey glared at Ardmore. He thought he saw something more than indignation there, but he could not be sure. Ramsey's frosty glance made Ardmore shiver in fear.

As Ramsey walked slowly past Helen, he stopped and said quietly, "Lyin' doesn't become a woman of your beauty." Then he marched ahead, back erect, eyes straight ahead.

He stopped when Burleson ordered him to do so. He turned to see Burleson telling the crowd to disperse. Off to the side, standing next to Ardmore, was Colin Weymouth. The Englishman was looking back at him, smirking.

Ramsey knew then that Weymouth had set this up, and that Ardmore and his daughter were in on it. He also vowed that he would make Weymouth pay for this. First, however, he would have to get out of jail. That might not be easy. The infraction, even if it had occurred, was a relatively minor one. But since it involved a young, innocent woman, people would not take it lightly. This could be far more severe than Ramsey was figuring on.

When he was locked in the cell in the sod jail house, he asked, "What's likely to happen, Sheriff?"

Burleson shrugged as he locked Ramsey's pistol and Winchester into a big wood chest against one wall. "You'll face Judge Waverly soon's he sees fit to hear the case. Most likely soon, since Ardmore carries some weight around Dirt Creek. After that . . ." he shrugged again.

Ramsey sat on the wood cot. This was, indeed turning into something more serious than he had imagined. On the face of it, he should get a day or two in jail and maybe have to pay a fine. They might even consider running him out of town. But it seemed that this was not a usual case.

He sighed and then smiled ruefully. He could not help but think that he not only had picked up Matt's knack for gunplay, he also seemed to have inherited a dose of his brother's bad luck, as Matt liked to call it.

Ramsey stretched out on the bed, hands behind his head, thinking. But he grew impatient. In a short while he rose and prowled around the small cell. He checked all the walls, wondering if there was a way to escape. He decided there was not. He knew the walls were made of sod and were about three feet thick. They were coated with several inches of hard adobe. With no tools to use, he would never be able to break through.

Just before dark, Cyrus Douglas arrived with a tray of food from Wohlford's Chop House. The thought was not very appealing, but Ramsey knew it would be all he would get.

As Douglas set the tray down, he whispered, "Things ain't so good fo' you, Mistah Ramsey." He glanced around to make sure Burleson was not paying too much attention. "Folks be talkin' po' 'bout you, and I heard Judge Wav'ly he plannin' to go hard on you."

"Thanks, Cyrus," Ramsey whispered back. "But I don't suppose there's a heap we can do about it."

"We'll see, Mistah Ramsey." Douglas flashed a quick grin and straightened up. "We'll see." He left and a bored Burleson locked the barred cell door behind him.

Douglas said nothing when he returned to pick up the dirty supper plates. He was quiet the next morning and noon, too. But at supper, he whispered, "He'p be comin' soon, Mistah Ramsey. Mebbe tomorra."

"What kind of help?"

"What the hell's goin' on in there, Cyrus?" Burleson demanded. "Just set his goddamn supper down and haul ass out of there, boy."

"Yassir." Douglas left with a small grin for Ramsey.

The jailed Texan had trouble sleeping that night. He wondered what Douglas had meant by help coming. He thought maybe that McFarrin had finally gotten sick of Weymouth and was planning to do something for Ramsey. That didn't seem likely, though it was the only thing Ramsey could think of. Unless Douglas was planning something, and that was a foolish thought.

Ramsey also had trouble sleeping because he was thinking of Eula Mae. His greatest regret about languishing here in this jail was not being able to tell her this was all some horrible error, that he was innocent. He knew Weymouth must be filling her head with all sorts of horrid tales about him, and that made Ramsey's stomach crawl with anger. *If only I could get word to her that I'm innocent*, he thought, *I'd be a happy man*.

He finally drifted off to sleep, thoughts of Eula Mae's sweet face and of revenge against Weymouth crowding into his brain.

CHAPTER
⋆10⋆

Eula Mae and Maybelle came to visit him in the afternoon. Ramsey was surprised, but mighty pleased, especially at seeing Eula Mae. She looked as beautiful as ever, though her face was creased by a frown of concern over him.

After a short visit with the two women standing outside the bars, Maybelle said, "Come on, Sheriff, let's step back into your office a spell. Let those young folk have a few moments of peace and privacy."

"Got to keep my eye on the prisoner, ma'am," Burleson said politely but sternly. "Make sure there's nothin' untoward goin' on."

"How could something untoward go on back there, what with him on one side of the bars and my granddaughter on the other?" She put a stern look on her old face, and the pipe bobbled. "Sheriff," Maybelle said with a sigh of annoyance. "We both know that Miss Helen Ardmore is little more than a tart. I'm powerful insulted that you'd lump that trollop and my granddaughter together in the same breath."

Burleson looked uncertain.

"And, sir, I resent the implication that my granddaughter is some sort of fallen woman that would resort to such unseemly behavior."

Burleson looked back over his shoulder at the prisoner. From behind him, Maybelle winked.

The lawman looked back at Maybelle. "I was referring to her maybe helpin' him try to escape, ma'am," he said blandly. He did not look at all abashed.

Maybelle's high-pitched cackle rose and floated around the room. "Pshaw, Sheriff," she chuckled. "My little girl over there breakin' the law and helpin' Mr. Ramsey escape?"

It did sound ludicrous, he had to admit. But he would admit it only to himself. Still, Artemis McFarrin was a respectable citizen of the area, and pretty well-off. Not so well-off as that hoity-toity Englishman, Colin Weymouth, maybe. But well-off enough to make his life miserable should he take a mind to.

"All right, ma'am," he said quietly. "But the door between my office and the cells here stays open."

"Agreed."

Burleson turned to face Ramsey and Eula Mae, who were holding hands through the bars. "You young folks best not try no funny business, you hear?"

Both nodded, and then Burleson and Maybelle strolled out into the office.

Ramsey had dozens of questions he wanted to ask, but he was having trouble getting started. It was enough that Eula Mae was here—and seemingly still in love with him.

Eula Mae broke the short silence. "We'll get you out of here tonight, Buck," she whispered after a look back to make sure the sheriff was not standing there.

"What?" he asked dumbfounded.

"You heard me." She was defiant and determined.

"But . . ."

"Shush and listen." She made another worried glance behind her. "Talk around town is that Judge Waverly's going to give you at least five years in the penitentiary." She shuddered involuntarily.

"He can't do . . ."

"Yes he can," Eula Mae hissed. "Colin has drummed up the people's hatred against you. A couple more days, and he'll have the whole town believing you ravished that lyin' little featherhead right there in the middle of the street." Her indignation was rising, as was her voice.

She managed to bring herself back down to a level of normalcy. "Anyway, that no good so-and-so has hinted to me that if the judge doesn't take care of you, he'll see to it that . . . well, there's always the rope, he's said more than once."

"That son of a . . ." Ramsey managed to bite off the rest of that oath.

"Here," Eula Mae said. She had been rummaging in her purse,

shielding her movements from the office with her body. Suddenly she produced a pistol and held it out just a little.

Ramsey took it and slid it into the waistband of his pants at the small of his back. He had not looked at it, other than to note it was a .38-caliber British Bulldog. It was a short, snub-nosed weapon that packed a pretty powerful punch.

"I don't want you usin' that on any townsfolk unless it's necessary," Eula Mae whispered. She might be stubborn and headstrong, but this was dangerous business, and she was getting worried. She did not want to be responsible for anyone's death.

"I won't," Ramsey promised. He would do whatever he needed to do.

"I give you that just in case we can't get you any other weapons," Eula Mae whispered. "Where are yours, in case we can get them?"

"The big box out there in the office. Under the rifle rack." He was certain there would be little chance to get the key to the box. Eula Mae nodded.

"You have a plan to get me out of here without me havin' to shoot anyone?"

"Yes."

"Time you was leaving, Miss Eula," Sheriff Burleson said. He came to the door. "You been here long enough."

"Yes, sir." Eula Mae turned and smiled sweetly at the lawman. "I'll be just a moment." Without waiting to see what the sheriff would do, Eula Mae leaned forward and kissed Ramsey through the bars. As their lips met, she whispered, "Just be ready tonight, Buck."

"I will," he answered before parting reluctantly from her. He watched her walk away. He was sad, but it was mixed with excitement as he thought about the possibility of escape.

As the sheriff escorted Eula Mae and Maybelle to the door, Ramsey quickly snatched out the Bulldog and jammed it into the top of his right boot. In the three seconds it took to do that, he considered just plugging Burleson in the back and breaking out of here now. But he had enough sense to know that would be an extremely foolish thing to do. It also would be highly dangerous for the two women. He could afford to wait a little while longer.

He lay down on the cot and pulled his hat over his eyes. Still, he was aware that Burleson had come back to check the cell door and then stood there for a few moments staring at him. Ramsey supposed the lawman had to make sure all was all right. He almost grinned at the thought of the pistol in his boot.

Ramsey wondered what the two women had cooked up to try to get him out of jail. Indeed, he wondered how they even knew what had happened. He knew they would have heard he had been arrested and was in jail, and they must have heard the story of how it happened. But they had shown every evidence in not believing that story. Either they knew the young woman in question and her father and discounted everything the two had to say, or someone had told them what had really happened.

He dozed off, and was awakened by Douglas, who was bringing his supper. The black man set the plates down, grinned surreptitiously and then left. Ramsey wondered about that, too, as he gnawed on the stringy, greasy chicken and slimy peas. The only things really edible were the biscuits, even though they were at least a week old.

When he finished, Ramsey forced himself to sit on the cot. He wanted to pace, to burn off some of the adrenaline-inspired energy that surged through him. But if he did so, he might make the sheriff suspicious. So he sat, waiting impatiently for something to happen.

He almost leaped out of his skin about two hours later when gunfire broke out in the street. Burleson, who was sitting in his chair sipping coffee, jumped up and bolted outside, leaving the door ajar.

A moment later, Eula Mae and Maybelle slipped into the room. Both smiled at Ramsey, who stood in his cell, watching. He returned the smiles. While the old woman kept a watch at the door, Eula Mae searched around the room. She finally found a crowbar propped in a corner. She grabbed it and jammed in through the lock on the box that held Ramsey's weapons. She pried with all her strength using the top of the box as a lever.

It snapped with a loud crack, and an accompanying short screech of surprise from Eula Mae.

At the same time, Ramsey spun around, dropping into a crouch and reaching for the Bulldog pistol in his boot. He had heard an odd, cracking sound from behind him. It came again and again, with a throbbing regularity. He crouched there in the cell, leaning back against the bars, wondering what the hell was going on and what was making the noise.

"Buck!" Eula Mae hissed from right behind him.

He turned, almost dazed by the turn of the events. Eula Mae

shoved his Winchester and his holstered Colt through the bars at him.

"Hurry, chil'," Maybelle called out.

"Yes'm." Eula Mae looked at Ramsey. "I'll see you outside soon."

"But how . . . ? Who . . . ?"

"Don't worry," Eula Mae said and ran for the door.

Ramsey was left to stand there, his befuddlement growing. He didn't have long to wait to find out what was happening, though. Suddenly the adobe and sod wall at the back of the cell produced a hole. Within moments, large chunks of the wall caved in.

The sweaty, grinning faces of Douglas and Jackson appeared in the hole. "Come on, Mistah Ramsey," Douglas said. "Time be a-wastin'."

Ramsey needed no further encouragement. He plunged through the wall, landing outside with a thump after he tripped on some chunks of sod. Douglas and Jackson were standing there with pickaxes in their hands.

Eula Mae and Maybelle were also there. And Biscuit was standing, saddled nearby, the reins tied to a bush.

"What're you two boys doin' here?" Ramsey asked, directing his question at the two blacks.

Jackson shuffled his feet on the ground. Douglas answered. "It was a payin' back for the he'p you give us that time over in the saloon."

"Skinner?"

"Yassir."

"Wasn't much I did."

"Fo' folks like us it was a heap." He looked ashamed, then found a reservoir of pride. " 'Sides, Mistah Ramsey, you's nearabout the only one ever treated us like jus' folks."

Ramsey nodded. He thought he could understand. "It was only right," he said. He looked at them questioning. "You boys ain't gonna get in no trouble over this, are you?"

"Nassir," Douglas said. "Me'n Solomon'll jus' disappear into town. Nobody'll ever know we was here." He grinned. "We brung yo' things from yo' room. It's all there on yo' hoss."

"Obliged, Cyrus. And to you, Solomon," Ramsey said. He meant every word. He shook the two men's hands, then shoved the Winchester into the saddle scabbard. Quickly he buckled on his gunbelt. He took a moment to make sure the pistol was loaded.

"Best get yourself a-movin', boy," Maybelle said urgently.

"Ride south, hard. I expect the sheriff'll have a posse after you before long. Eventually swing around west and work back up toward the ranch. There's an old soddy up along Horse Creek, maybe six miles from the house. It's in pretty good shape. Some of the hands use it as a line camp at times. There's a spring nearby. Hole up there."

"For how long?" Ramsey asked as he swung up onto Biscuit.

"Me and Eula Mae'll come for you."

"Ride safely, Buck," Eula Mae said.

"You'll be all right, Eula?" Ramsey asked. He was suddenly worried about her.

"Yes. Now go."

"And you, Miz Maybelle?"

"I'll be fine, soon's you get outta here so's me and Eula can get home without raisin' suspicions. Now, ride, boy."

Ramsey nodded. He knew it as well as anyone. He slapped Biscuit with his hat, and the horse raced off. He looked back only once, a minute later. His four rescuers were already gone.

As he cleared the south end of town, almost riding over a drunk wandering up the street, Ramsey thought he heard Sheriff Burleson shouting and bellowing. Ramsey figured a posse would not be long in forming.

CHAPTER
★11★

It was one hell of an exciting ride, Ramsey thought later: racing through the starlit night, not knowing if Biscuit might step in a chuck hole or something and kill the both of them.

But he could not slacken his speed, at least not for a while. The land here was too flat, and offered no place to hide and let the posse pass him by. He had the fleeting thought that he wished he were back up in the mountains, which Kyle had called home for so many years. He thought he could finally understand—and appreciate—some of the qualities of living in the high lonesome. Up there, in most places, he would be able to hide within a hundred yards of town and no one would be able to find him.

But there was no use in worrying about such things now. He had to put some distance between himself and the soon-to-follow posse.

He was glad that Biscuit was well-rested. Old Em Fortney over at the livery stable had been taking real good care of the ginger-colored horse. The animal had been well-fed and well-watered there. And, the stallion was a tough, sturdy prairie mustang. He might be fairly short, but he was hardy and had a massive chest that gave him long wind. The horse would be able to run all night, if need be.

Ramsey hoped that would not be necessary. He ran the horse almost flat-out for fifteen or twenty minutes, before easing back some. The steed seemed to enjoy the run more than the rider had. Ramsey kept Biscuit at a steady gallop for another hour. Then he eased off some more, moving at a graceful canter.

He figured it was about midnight when he finally pulled to a stop. He dismounted and loosened his saddle, letting Biscuit breathe for a while. He looked back on his trail, but even with the almost full moon spreading its brightness over the land, he could see nothing. He thought he could hear the sound of running horses, but he thought it might just be his imagination.

He waited impatiently, knowing the horse would need some time. But finally he figured he would need to get on the trail again. He had put some distance between him and the posse; he didn't want to let them close up the gap. He tightened the saddle and swung himself up into it.

Ramsey kept up a steady pace through the night, moving on for some miles before stopping to let the horse rest. He found that someone—he assumed Eula Mae and Maybelle—had put some beef jerky and biscuits in a sack and had tied it to the saddle. He took some time at one point to eat some of both, while Biscuit grazed nearby.

Then he was riding again. He didn't know how far he had come from Dirt Creek when dawn broke, but he estimated it was thirty or so miles. He hoped the posse had gotten discouraged. But he could not take the chance of turning northward until he was certain. He did swing west, though, moving at a slow but steady pace.

Ramsey stopped atop a knoll just before daybreak. He loosened Biscuit's saddle—again. He began to feel like that's all he had done for the past week or so, tighten and loosen his saddle. He took his small sack of supplies and sat. There was no coffee, but he had a full canteen of water. He sat, gnawing on jerky and hard biscuits while he watched the morning begin along his back trail.

An overwhelming desire to sleep enveloped him, but he knew he could not give in to it. He forced himself to stand and walk around a little and then splashed some water on his face. It helped some. He turned back to face the east.

That's when he spotted signs of the posse for the first time. A hanging cloud of dust was drifting in his direction. It moved slowly; from Ramsey's position on the knoll, it seemed to be moving reluctantly. Ramsey nodded. He took his time packing his few things, and then cinched his saddle. He seemed in no hurry as he moseyed up the trail. He figured the posse would be at least as tired as he, maybe more so.

By noon, though, Ramsey's tiredness—and therefore his irritation—was growing along with the sun and temperature. He was tired of running, tired of being followed. He decided he would put an end to it one way or another.

Half an hour later, Ramsey found another short knoll. He rode to the top of it, and looked back. He could see for miles eastward. There was not a tree nor bush, neither gully nor ridge. His followers would have no cover. He could pick them off at his leisure, should he choose to do so.

Ramsey figured he wouldn't have to go that far. It would only cause more trouble later. He fully intended to ride back into Dirt Creek one day and see that his name was cleared of the ridiculous charges that had been leveled at him. If he was to kill a couple of citizens of Dirt Creek in cold blood, though, there would be no going back. Ever. There would be a price on his head, too. He didn't want that, since that would mean he and Eula Mae would not be able to live their lives in peace. He planned to make Eula Mae his as soon as he possibly could.

So, he thought, killing a couple posse men outright was not a very good idea. But that did not mean he could not do what was necessary to discourage the temporary lawmen following him.

Ramsey unsaddled Biscuit completely this time, dropping the saddle near the eastern side of the knoll. After tossing the saddle blanket next to it, he took some time in rubbing the horse down. The animal had pulled him through some hard times, and deserved the best treatment possible. Right now that treatment might not be great, but Ramsey would do what he could.

When he finished, Ramsey went to his saddle and sat next to it. He pulled the Winchester from the saddle scabbard and checked it over. He had cleaned it not long before Sheriff Burleson had taken it from him, and it had not been used since. He made sure the magazine was full, and set his box of extra cartridges next to the saddle.

He stood and stretched, trying to ease some of the tiredness. It helped some. He looked east. The cloud was growing nearer, but it was moving slower and still was some miles off.

He sat again and finished off his jerky and hard biscuits. Then he took the horse across the knoll and tied him to a picket ring he had pounded into the ground. The horse, just over the crown of the mound, should be pretty well-protected from any stray bullets.

He went back to his saddle and looked out. The posse was only half a mile away. Ramsey grabbed his rifle and stretched out behind the saddle. It was the only cover he would have. Sliding the Winchester over the seat, he waited.

He fired when the posse was still at least three hundred yards away. He deliberately placed the three shots short, not wanting to risk hitting anyone—yet.

The posse pulled up short and fast. They bounced around as confusion began to take over.

Up on the ridge, Ramsey could hear Burleson yelling, trying to bring the men under control. *He's a cool one, that sheriff is*, Ramsey thought.

Not to be too taken in by Burleson's calmness under fire, Ramsey let loose two more shots, bringing them in a little closer to the posse, but still not too close. The two shots served to keep the confusion stirred up.

Ramsey lay back and waited, while Burleson shouted and roared. Eventually he brought the men under some semblance of control.

The posse moved on, more slowly, spreading out. At about two hundred fifty yards, Ramsey shouted, "You've come far enough, boys." He looked over the saddle and saw that the men had stopped.

"That you, Ramsey?" Burleson called.

"Yep."

"You're in a heap of trouble already, boy," Burleson shouted. "Don't make it worse. Give yourself up peaceable and nothing'll happen to you."

"And let you take me back to Dirt Creek? No, sir, Sheriff." He paused. "Not with a lynch mob waitin' for me back there."

"Where'd you ever get such a notion, boy?"

"I got a few friends in Dirt Creek."

"There ain't no lynch mob, Ramsey. Now give yourself up and let's be done with all this."

"No. Now, I got no hankerin' to kill any of you folks. But I ain't going back. Not with a posse. You let things settle down and get folks back there to listen to some sense, and I'll come on in on my own. Till then, though, I expect you best head on back before someone gets hurt."

Burleson turned to his men and said something that Ramsey could not hear at his distance. Suddenly all the men in the posse spurred their horses forward.

"Hell and damnation," Ramsey muttered. He snapped the rifle up and pumped out six quick shots. The first two he deliberately put into the ground; the next four took down horses. He was still reluctant to shoot anyone, but he had to stop them, and soon. They were within two hundred yards.

Four horses went down in a sprawl of legs. Riders went flying, bouncing in the dirt and grass. Ramsey hoped none of them was hurt too seriously.

The others pulled up, panic seeming to set in. Even Burleson stopped and slid out of his saddle. He began shouting orders again, but this time Ramsey could not really make any words out, considering the noise of horses and almost a dozen men shouting at the same time.

Ramsey took advantage of the respite to fill the magazine of his rifle. He did so by rote, without looking. Instead, he kept his eyes on the posse. By the time the Winchester was reloaded, Burleson had whipped his men into some form of order again. One was holding the good horses, moving them back a little way. Several others were helping the four who had been thrown; the rest were lying flat behind the dead horses.

"Like I said, Sheriff," Ramsey shouted, "I'm not hankerin' to kill anyone."

"Then drop that rifle and come along," Burleson insisted.

"Like hell. Now listen, Sheriff. I didn't do nothin' to that girl, and I expect you damn well know it. Even if I had done what they said, it ain't worth a posse like this and all this grief."

Burleson was silent for a while, thinking. Ramsey was right, of course, he knew. He wasn't absolutely certain that Ramsey hadn't taken some liberties with Helen Ardmore, but even if he had, it wasn't worth getting somebody killed for. Still, he had set out to do a job. It was not like him to quit with the job unfinished.

"You'll have to face the judge for the trouble you've wrought here, Ramsey," he said. *Maybe I can bring him in that way,* he thought. "You damned near killed two of these men; the other two ain't so bad off."

"If I wanted 'em dead, Sheriff, they'd be dead," Ramsey shouted. "I hit what I aim at. You ask around folks who know me. There ain't a better shot with a rifle than me."

"Damn," Burleson spat quietly. *He's got me there, too,* he thought. He also believed Ramsey on that point. He lay there, thinking. There were two problems in not bringing Ramsey back, as far as he could see. For one, it would leave him feeling like he had failed to do his job. And the second, he'd have one hell of a time trying to explain it to Judge Waverly—and Weymouth, Ardmore, and anyone else who had a stake in all this.

He looked at his men. One looked in fairly bad shape. The other three would make it. He figured that Shavely, though, would need a doctor's care, and the sooner the better.

"Don't come back to Dirt Creek, Ramsey," Burleson bellowed, trying to make it sound threatening. He hoped Ramsey would take the hint.

"I ain't makin' no promises, Sheriff." Ramsey knew Burleson was trying to save face, and he understood that. But he also wanted the lawman to know that he could not be pushed too far. However, he didn't want to make the sheriff's job any harder. The harder he made it for Burleson, the more trouble Burleson might cause eventually. So he added, "But I ain't makin' any plans to visit again, either."

Burleson knew he would get no better out of this. His only worry now was that Ramsey might shoot one of his men as they were leaving. Then he realized that was ridiculous. Ramsey had never done anything of the sort, not that he knew of. He stood, and called to the man holding the horses. The man warily began bringing the animals closer.

"Some of you boys get Shavely on a horse. Bracus, you ride up behind him, hold him on. Move out as fast as you can. Shavely needs to get to the doc soon's possible."

"What about us?" one man asked.

"Some of you can either double up. Or walk," Burleson said harshly. He still felt twinges of guilt at leaving a job undone. But there was nothing he could do about it now. Still, he didn't have to feel good about it, nor did he have to stand here and listen to anyone whine.

Up on the mound, Ramsey lay behind his saddle, Winchester ready. He watched alertly. Once he had seen Burleson stand, he knew the sheriff and the posse would be leaving. He did worry a little, however, that one of the posse men might take it into his head to take a few parting shots at him. So he waited.

CHAPTER

★ 12 ★

Ramsey stood up when the posse was out of rifle range. He stood there, watching, until the new cloud of traveling dust was a mere blur on the horizon. With his rifle still in hand, Ramsey wandered down to where the posse had been brought to a stop.

Already the buzzards were gathering in the air currents. They glided silently on the drifts, squawking occasionally. One of the four horses Ramsey had shot was still alive, struggling feebly. Not wanting to see the animal suffer, Ramsey shot the horse in the head.

Then Ramsey poked around, looking for anything that might be of use to him. The posse men had taken all four saddles, but in the confusion, one set of saddlebags had been left behind, as had several burlap or canvas sacks. It was to those that Ramsey gravitated right off.

He looked through the bags and came up with a little chunk of smoked beef, a small pouch of coffee, a large coffeepot, a handful of beans, and several small hunks of days-old bread, wrapped in paper. For Ramsey, who had run out of food, it was a real find.

He marched back up the small hill and looked back. There was no sign that the posse had turned around. Ramsey put the new food things down and then wandered around gathering up as much booshwa as he could find and carted it back to his "camp."

He decided not to bother digging a fire pit. He simply stacked a pile of the cow chips up and lit them with a match. With the fire going, he poured about half the water from his canteen into the coffeepot, added some coffee, and set it on the flames to boil. There wasn't much he could do with the beans, so he left them in the sack. He jammed his knife into the piece of smoked meat and propped it over the flames with a couple of rocks. Then he leaned back against his saddle to wait for his meal to be done. He fought off sleep, keep a watchful eye to the east, just in case the posse decided to come back.

Finally he ate half the meat and two pieces of the hard, crunchy bread. It wasn't the best meal he ever had, but it was filling. He appreciated the coffee most, though.

After his meal, he sat watching the plains to the east and thinking about his predicament. He had been in worse situations, far worse. But for some reason, this one seemed somehow more annoying. He was lonely and frustrated. The whole world seemed to be conspiring against him, and it was not a pleasant thought.

He half wished that Matt or Kyle were with him. On the other hand, he wouldn't wish this miserable outing on anyone. Besides, he figured there wasn't much they'd be able to do that he couldn't do himself.

That, however, was much of his problem. He didn't seem to be able to do anything to solve his problems, which were many. First off, there was Eula Mae. He loved her and wanted her. He was certain she wanted him, too. But they didn't seem to be able to get together. Not even so much as five minutes alone since he had been up this way. He needed to talk with her, settle things, see where he—and she—stood. When and how they could do that was another problem.

A more serious trouble was presented by Colin Weymouth. Ramsey knew the Englishman was up to no good, but he could not figure out what it was. All he knew was that whatever Weymouth was up to, it did not bode well for Eula Mae or her family. They were all somehow connected in all this.

Making the situation worse, Ramsey knew for absolute certain that Weymouth had engineered his arrest and imprisonment. He had assumed at first that it was simply to keep him away from Eula Mae for a while, so that Weymouth could have a clear field at courting her. But in his long ride fleeing from Dirt Creek, he had begun to suspect there was a more sinister reason behind it. He also began to realize that this, too, was tied up in whatever scheme Weymouth was hatching, that Weymouth wanted him out of the way to do whatever it was he was contemplating.

Such thoughts only added to Ramsey's exasperation. Until he knew what Weymouth was up to, there was little he could do to stop it. He had never felt so helpless in all his life. Such feelings made his anger and exasperation grow.

Those feelings also made his loneliness grow. He felt a need to talk with someone. Not just anyone, but someone he could trust. Like Matt, or even Kyle, though his one-armed brother often seemed distant from him. His two big brothers might josh with him over his troubles with women and such, but they had all been through the same things—and worse—and would listen and offer him counsel, based on their own experiences.

Sleep threatened to overtake him, and he angrily forced himself up. "Damn," he muttered. He did not like feeling this way at all, did not like letting his emotions getting the better of him.

He took a last glance toward the east. Dusk was rising there, dimming the lush prairie lands that stretched endlessly for miles and miles. But he could see no one was coming for him. Still, he felt a little uneasy staying here like this. If the posse was figuring on coming back under cover of night, they would know just where he could be found. He could not have that.

Ramsey forced himself to move. He stomped out what little remained of the fire and stowed away his few supplies. Then he saddled Biscuit and rode out, heading northwest.

He went only about a mile or so, until he found another knoll. Like the other, it was treeless, and swept by a constant breeze. But it did give him a panorama for some miles in all directions. He unsaddled the horse again and set his saddle down. With one last look around, he spread out his bedroll, and lay down.

As tired as he was, he still had some trouble getting to sleep, what with all the problems, worries, and concerns plaguing him. But he eventually dozed off, and then fell into a deep sleep.

The sun was fairly high when he awoke. He stood and stretched. He felt considerably better than he had, and he realized that half his worries had been brought about by his exhaustion. He still had no answers to the problems that confronted him—and those problems certainly were real enough—but he no longer felt so helpless. He didn't know what he would do to set things to right, but he was filled with his usual self-confidence. He would set them right, somehow.

He checked on Biscuit, and then stood for a few moments turning in a circle, looking out over the plains. No one was in sight. With somewhat renewed spirits, he set about making breakfast. He finished off the smoked meat and bread, but went sparingly on the coffee and water from his canteen. He had precious little of each left. He figured he could always hunt for meat, but without water, he would not last too long.

The small fire of buffalo and cow chips burned hot, bright, and pungently, if briefly. He did not need its heat, but he found that the crackling flames, dancing in the wind, comforted him a little. But soon enough he figured he had better get on the trail.

His first order of business, he decided, was to find water, if any was available out here. The second would be to hunt. The third, get to that old soddy as quickly as possible. Once he had done that, he would wait on Eula Mae and Maybelle. Then he could try to find out what was going on and how he could best help.

Pushed on by a growing sense of urgency, he hurriedly packed away what little supplies he had left. He saddled Biscuit and rode off, cutting almost straight north now.

Around noon, with the sun hanging high overhead and the heat nearly enough to smother a body, he polished off the last of the water from his canteen. An hour later, he began to worry that he might not find any more. His mouth was dry, though his shirt was soaked from sweat. He pressed on, figuring the horse must be suffering even more than he.

Desperation grew through the afternoon. The heat and worry spawned a fear that he would never be able to find any water. It began to prey on his mind, until he thought he would go crazy.

His hopes soared once, as he rode down into a stream bed. They crashed when he realized the steam bed was as dry as his throat. "Shit," he mumbled, voice thickened by thirst. He rode on, urging the horse up the other side of the bank and forward.

His mind played some tricks on him after that, until he stopped and stared ahead briefly, his anger growing. He roared out his annoyance. It didn't solve his problem, but it did serve to bring him back to his senses a little. He turned the horse and rode back to the dry stream bed. There might not be any water, but there was some shade in the brush and with the suffering cottonwoods. It helped ease the heat more than a little. He unsaddled Biscuit and rubbed him down before letting the horse free to graze. Ramsey hoped the grass and cottonwood shoots would provide some water for the steed.

Ramsey popped a pebble in his mouth to try to work up a little spit. With the faint hope that he might find some underground water, he jabbed his knife into the sand of the stream bottom and began digging. All he found, though, was a little damp sand. He scooped up a handful and squeezed it over his other hand. He managed to force out a few drops of liquid. Eagerly, he wiped the gritty dampness off his hand with his tongue.

A dozen times, he repeated the process. It didn't do much to really allay his thirst, but it did wet his lips and mouth a fraction, enough to let him relax a little. It gave him confidence that he might pull through—if he found some real water soon.

Ramsey lay in the shade of a cottonwood, his head resting on his saddle. He pulled his hat over his eyes and dozed fitfully. He roused himself after the sun had gone down. He went back to the hole, dug out several more handfuls of damp sand and squeezed out just enough moisture to wet his lips again.

Without hurry, he saddled Biscuit and rode slowly out. With the sun gone, the heat had dissipated, and the ride was considerably less trying. The moon's brightness was obscured occasionally by clouds, but for the most part, it provided enough light to see by as he rode along the mainly flat prairie.

Still, he had found no real water source by dawn. An hour after sunrise, he found another shady gully that might at times have water in it. He stopped and made a camp, such as it was. His only food was two jackrabbits he shot just before stopping. He gathered a little wood and made a small fire. He dangled one rabbit over the fire on a stick. Like most of the men he knew, he preferred his meat seared almost black, but this time, he let the meat get barely warm before he began eating it. The rabbit was stringy, but was fairly juicy.

He felt a little better after eating, what with the meager moisture he had consumed from it. He began to worry about the horse, though. The animal had had no real water in a few days. There was little Ramsey could really do about it, other than to hope the mount had gotten some moisture from the grass he had been eating—and from the dew that had collected on the grass here in the shady gully.

Ramsey dug down into the dirt again, hoping he might find a little more moisture since this was grass-covered ground, rather than mostly bare sand. He dug a small hole about two feet deep, but found little damp soil. He squeezed a bit of moisture out for himself, and then covered the hole with his saddlebags. If any water at all gathered, he hoped the cover would prevent evaporation.

Then he stretched out on his blankets, hat covering his face. He slept uneasily.

He was awakened by the rain on his face. At first he thought he was dreaming. Then he realized it was really rain. He lay there, mouth open, trying to let some rainwater in, for a time. As the rain increased in intensity, however, it began to dawn on him that he was in a prime place to be engulfed by a flash flood.

He rose and kicked the saddlebags away from the hole. He pulled on his slicker and rolled up his canvas-and-blanket bedroll. By that time, the hole was filled with water. He brought Biscuit over and let the animal drink, though he suspected the horse had already drank some from whatever puddles had already formed. But this gave the animal at least one long drink.

Before saddling the horse, Ramsey set his hat down on the ground upside down. The rain felt good on his bare head. He took the hat and poured the water as carefully as he could into his canteen; then, he set the hat down to collect more water while he let Biscuit empty the hole of water again.

The second hatful of water was almost enough to fill the canteen halfway. He slapped the hat on, tied his bedroll behind the saddle and then filled the canteen from the hole. He mounted up and rode on. He enjoyed this rain more than he ever had enjoyed such a thing.

It was still raining when he pulled to a stop late in the afternoon. He was afraid to make his camp in any gully, worried that a flash flood might come along. So he had no real protection from the rain. He didn't much care, though. The rain might be annoying at times, but after his thirst, he didn't mind it at all.

CHAPTER
13

Early in the afternoon, two days later, Ramsey found the soddy. He sat out on the flat prairie two hundred yards away for a while, watching. He just wanted to make sure no one was there. He had seen no one at all since he had chased the posse off several days ago, but one could never be too careful, he figured.

It had stopped raining the day before, and this day was clear and warm. All thoughts of his thirst were gone, washed away by the day and a half of pounding storms.

He finally began moving. But rather than heading straight toward the old sod house, he moved parallel to it, walking Biscuit slowly. He took in the scenery as he rode, following the muddy bank of the almost dry Horse Creek, then crossing it and curling around the soddy. He wanted to see the house from all angles, as well as to make sure there was no one hiding somewhere behind the brush, or on the ridge off a ways. And, for all he knew, there might still be someone in the house waiting to take a shot at him.

The soddy was built under the leafy branches of two large cottonwoods. Just to the right of the house as he faced it origi-nally was the spring Maybelle had mentioned, a bubbling pool surrounded by brush and brambles. There was a knoll behind the house, but not close enough to present too much of a danger to anyone inside.

As promised, the soddy was in pretty good condition for one that had not been used regularly. One wall—the one opposite the spring—had one big, gaping hole in it. But from what Ramsey could see the roof and the rest of the walls were intact. That was a little surprising, considering the heavy rains of the past couple of days.

When he had completely circled the soddy, he decided it was time to ride on in. He had seen nothing that would indicate to him that anyone had been there since the rain. It was still possible, of course, that someone had come along a couple of days ago and was still waiting inside the house. But he would have to go to the soddy sooner or later. Still, he was tense as he turned Biscuit's head toward the shack.

No gunfire erupted from inside, and Ramsey stopped right outside it. He dismounted and loosened Biscuit's saddle. With a sigh of resignation, he headed for the front door. He was always reluctant to enter such a place—rats, snakes, and God only knows what else most likely had had free rein in the place for some time, and that would mean some housecleaning with his six-gun. He was not afraid of snakes, but he had no liking for them, either. Nor did he take kindly to rats. And, there was always the danger that one of them would get him before he got them. So he was uncomfortable in entering the soddy, but it had to be done.

Someone had lined the doorway with old wood and then hammered some rusty hinges to the framing and hung a rickety old outhouse door. It looked odd, with its half-moon letting in some of the light. Ramsey wondered why anyone had bothered, since with the hole in one wall and the uncovered windows, the door would do nothing to keep out unwanted guests.

He shoved the door open, and stood in the entrance a few moments. Then he entered slowly, moving in just a few steps, Colt pistol in hand. He emptied the pistol at a nest of snakes in one corner.

He walked farther into the house's only room, leaving the door open behind him. Between the door, the holes in the one wall and the window on each side, there was a fair amount of light in the place. With the light, Ramsey could see that there were two cots along the back wall, a large table of thick wood slabs and three matching chairs, an old Franklin stove, a tilting cupboard with coffeepot, cups, and plates. There were two coal-oil lanterns— one on the table, one on the cupboard.

Ramsey went to the table and lifted that lantern. He shook it, relieved when he heard it sloshing with fuel. He scraped a match on the table and held it to the wick and then eased the glass chimney down. Light flooded the room, dispelling the darkness that had lurked in the corners.

The place looked a little more inviting with the light thrown by the lantern, even if it was a harsh yellow glare. He blasted two rats and another rattlesnake. Only somewhat squeamishly, he picked up the dead critters and tossed them out the door. He was a little surprised at seeing so few pests inside the cabin.

That mystery was somewhat cleared up when he took a closer look around the inside. It was evident that someone had been here, and not too long ago. There were blankets on the cots; the plates, cups, and coffeepot were mostly clean; the wood box next to the stove was full; and he even found some food in the cupboard.

He wasn't sure who had left the items. Maybelle had said that some of the ranch hands used the soddy as a line shack at times, and it could've been left by them. Or, Maybelle and Eula Mae could've been out here looking for him and brought the items. Either way, he was glad to see the things, especially the food.

Ramsey brought Biscuit inside and unsaddled him. He threw the saddle on a chair and then curried him. Next to the cupboard was a sack of grain. He opened the bag and poured some into an old bucket for the horse. He didn't particularly like having the horse inside with him, but he felt it necessary, at least for now. He did not want anyone passing by to see the animal tied outside. He wanted to remain as hidden as possible until he talked with Eula Mae and Maybelle and decided what to do.

That done, he tossed some kindling in the small, flat-topped parlor-model cookstove, fired it up, and then patiently added large pieces of wood until he had a good blaze going. He fixed up coffee in the pot and set that on the stove. Then he set beans to cooking in a pot and bacon in a frying pan. He sat back to wait for his meal.

After eating more than he should have, he went outside and walked around. He wanted to get the lay of the land settled in his head, and he felt the need for some fresh air.

Darkness was beginning to fall, and he was getting tired anyway, so after a short walk, he headed back inside. He stretched out on one cot, grateful for its meager comfort. He pulled the blanket around him and fell asleep almost instantly.

Eula Mae and Maybelle showed up early the next afternoon. Ramsey, sitting inside sipping coffee, heard the clattering of the carriage from half a mile off. Grabbing the Winchester, he stood and headed for one of the windows. When he saw who it was, he smiled in relief before stepping outside to await their arrival.

Eula Mae fairly tumbled out of the carriage before it was stopped and rushed to him. Ramsey was a little embarrassed as he returned Eula Mae's avid hugs and kisses under the tolerant gaze of old Maybelle. The old lady sat, teeth gripping the pipe while she grinned like mad.

Finally, the two young people broke off their embrace. "I was so worried about you," Eula Mae said breathlessly. "We expected you here days ago."

"Got in yesterday," Ramsey said. His joy was almost boundless, but he was making a manly effort to keep it concealed. "Took me a little longer'n I figured to ditch that posse."

"Any trouble?" Eula Mae asked, suddenly afraid for him.

"None to speak of." He paused. He certainly was not about to tell her he almost died of thirst. But he felt she would need to be told something, and he felt that telling her as much truth as possible under the circumstances might be best. "I wouldn't of had no trouble gettin' away from those boys if I hadn't minded blastin' a couple of them."

"Why didn't you?" Eula Mae asked, innocently. She was angry that Ramsey had been put in this position in the first place. Defending himself wasn't the worst thing he could do.

"Would've made everything worse," Ramsey said evenly. He explained his thoughts on it.

"Smart thinkin', boy," Maybelle said as she climbed down from the wagon. She stretched, wincing a little. Her age was catching up to her, but she hated to admit it, even to herself.

She placed her hands against the small of her back and rubbed as she walked toward Eula Mae and Ramsey. "You found the food we left all right?" she asked, stopping. Her bones ached like never before. It was from too much riding in the carriage, she knew.

She sighed. She was too old for such things. She ought to be back at the ranch house, sitting in her rocking chair, taking her leisure. If only her son-in-law had any gumption, she thought sourly, she would be. However, she at least had that to look forward to, she figured. As soon as Buck Ramsey cleared up this mess, she could get back to her rocker.

"Yes'm. I'm obliged." Ramsey looked almost ashamed. Having to be rescued from jail by an old lady, the woman he loved and two poor black men ate at him. He knew, though, that such help should be acknowledged. "I'm obliged to you—both of you—for helpin' me out back in Dirt Creek." He swallowed hard. Eating humble pie wasn't easy for a prideful man such as he was.

"Weren't nothin'," Maybelle said. She was beginning to feel a little better. "It was the least we could do after all you've done for us."

"Hell," Ramsey muttered, still ashamed.

Maybelle grinned. "I expect you two young folks have a heap to discuss after so long a spell apart," she said quietly. "And I expect I need to walk some, stretch out these old legs of mine." She winked, almost shocking the lovebirds. "I reckon half an hour ought to be long enough to work up my circulation."

Ramsey was not sure the old woman was saying what he thought she was saying. He looked at her in some disbelief. She nodded back, still grinning.

Ramsey looked down at Eula Mae, who was staring up at him. A smile was on her lips, and love was in her eyes. But it seemed fear placed a sheen over her whole face. He realized it was fear of his rejection. He smiled at her. "You certain?" he whispered.

Eula Mae nodded, eyes eager. She touched his arm and headed for the door.

Just before Ramsey turned to follow Eula Mae, Maybelle came up and said quietly, "It's all right, Buck. When I was a girl, people didn't think quite so poor of such things. Besides, the way things've been of late . . ."

Maybelle wandered off as a dazed Ramsey watched for a few moments. The old lady went to the carriage, where she rooted out her small bottle of spirits. She took a nip and then wandered down toward the spring, smiling to herself, remembering forty-some years ago, when she was young and spry, when a young, strong man named Caleb Sweet was bedding her in their old soddy down in Texas. Times were precious then, though they had nothing but each other. She missed those times, certain, but she was glad she could let her granddaughter and her beau find some of those precious times of their own.

Ramsey was no longer watching Maybelle. He had turned and gone into the house, where an eager Eula Mae awaited him.

Ramsey grumbled when Maybelle rapped on the door. Instead of a half hour, it seemed as if only minutes had passed. But he realized she would not have come back too early. He rose hurriedly and stumbled into his clothes.

Moments later, Eula Mae did the same. She managed to give Ramsey one last long look at her before she was fully covered and patting her hair in place.

Ramsey opened the door, and Maybelle came in. She went straight to the stove. She nodded when she saw that Ramsey had coffee on. She poured cups for all of them, liberally dosing

Ramsey's with whiskey. She also poured a much smaller portion of liquor for herself.

The three sat at the table and sipped a few moments. Finally Ramsey asked, "All right, ladies, exactly what's goin' on?"

"Nothing right now," Eula Mae said with a giggle. Her eyes flashed brightly.

Maybelle looked over at her granddaughter and smiled warmly. The girl's cheeks fairly glowed and she had a healthy, loved look about her. Maybelle could remember feeling like that and was happy that Eula Mae had had the experience of it.

Ramsey grew angry for a moment. Then he grinned at Eula Mae's little joke. "We could change that, you know . . ." He blushed.

Eula Mae giggled some more, and Maybelle guffawed.

When they had all quieted again, Ramsey said, "Seriously, now, I need to know what's goin' on."

Maybelle nodded. "It's not all that hard to tell, though some of it does seem a mite strange, I suppose." She filled her pipe with tobacco and lit it. As she was doing so, she said, "Fetch us more coffee, girl."

Eula Mae refilled their cups and sat again.

As Maybelle talked, she made sucking sounds around the stem of the pipe. Rather than distracting the other two, it seemed somehow homey to them.

CHAPTER
★ 14 ★

"Colin Weymouth wants the ranch," Maybelle said evenly, though Ramsey could hear a tinge of anger deep down.

"I figured that much, Miz Maybelle. Though he ain't ever said nothin' in my hearin' about it, he ain't exactly hidden that desire either." He paused. "What I don't know is *why* he wants it so bad. That's the important thing, I'd expect."

"Told you he was no fool, Granny," Eula Mae said, sticking out her tongue playfully at her grandmother.

"Hush, girl," Maybelle said. But it was said affectionately. She turned her gaze on Ramsey. "Mr. Weymouth has struck a deal with the Midland Central Railroad," Maybelle said.

Ramsey sat there looking bewildered. "But there ain't no railroad around here," he said, trying to understand.

Maybelle smiled like a cat in the cream. "That's the thing. The Midland Central folk want to bring the railroad through a portion of the Big Horizon."

"Reckon bringin' the railroad through these parts makes plenty of sense. But why on Big Horizon land?" Ramsey asked, still perplexed. "Why not just run it through Dirt Creek? Town's already there. I got to admit it ain't much of a town, but it's there and waitin'."

Maybelle smiled. "That Weymouth is a sly fox, he is. Oh yes." Maybelle paused to relight her pipe and sip a little coffee. "He—and the railroad—aim to skip Dirt Creek." She beamed at the look of surprise on Ramsey's face.

"What'n hell would he want to do that for?" Ramsey asked. It made absolutely no sense for Weymouth, or the railroad officials, for that matter, to want to bypass Dirt Creek.

"Does seem foolish, don't it?" Maybelle asked. When Ramsey nodded, she said simply, "Water."

Ramsey looked at her with a question in his eye.

"There's a spot on the ranch that Weymouth's got his eye on, covetous villain that he is. It's got a real good water supply. It'll make a fine spot for a train station."

"And a town?" Ramsey asked, thinking he saw some answers looming.

"And a town," Maybelle said with a nod. She looked at Eula Mae and grinned. "You were right, girl. He is fair smart."

"And you wanted me not to wait for him," Eula Mae said with a mock pout.

"Pshaw," Maybelle snorted with a raspy chuckle. "I was the one told you he'd be back one day."

Ramsey sat listening to the fond banter, wondering how the two women could be so joyful when they all faced so many problems. There was still so much to be answered. But he forced himself to relax and let the interchange wind down. When the two women were looking at him again, he said, "But why not use Dirt Creek? It's got water."

"Not enough to fill train boilers regular."

That made sense to Ramsey. A train could consume a vast quantity of water. If they were running regular, a sure, steady supply was needed.

"Besides," Maybelle added, "in addition, puttin' the train across the Big Horizon Ranch will put the railroad a little closer to most of the ranches in the area, so it'll be easier to ship cattle eastward. Won't have to have no long drives, walkin' meat off the steers."

Ramsey's nod acknowledged the wisdom of it. Still, something didn't seem right to him, but it wouldn't come to him right now. "Where is this Eden?" he asked.

"Southwest of the house," Maybelle answered. "A fine little place it is, too. A crick, good-size spring, cottonwoods, some ashes, and honeylocusts."

"About four, five miles from the house?"

"Yep."

Ramsey nodded. "I've seen it. It'd be a fine spot for a town." He fell silent for a few moments. Then he finally realized what had not seemed right to him. "Don't the folks in Dirt Creek mind that the railroad won't be goin' through town?" he asked. He thought that strange. People all over the West fought to have the railroad located in their town. It meant a better economy, more business, an improved life for almost everyone. He could not picture people in a dirt-poor town like Dirt Creek not fighting to have the railroad come through there.

"They still think the railroad's coming through town, not bypassin' it by a couple of miles. Mr. Weymouth"—the name was said with a healthy dose of disdain—"has not disabused them of the notion."

"Why ain't you and Mr. McFarrin passed word around town? Weymouth seems to be getting a heap of help from the folks in Dirt Creek. They knew he was conspirin' against them, they might not be so friendly toward him."

"We just found that out recent." Maybelle shook her head in annoyance. "He's a slick one, that boy is. Why, I swear, he could sell coal to ol' Beelzebub himself. Apparently he's told those folks the railroad *will* be coming through town and that he's plannin' on buyin' lots of land and all in the area, and that he'll help promote the town with folks back East. They believe it, and so they're willing to help that skunk."

"Callin' him a skunk's too good for him," Ramsey muttered. He stood and paced, trying to sort it all out.

"Amen," Eula Mae whispered.

Ramsey stopped and stared at the young woman. She was the most beautiful woman he had ever seen, always had been. He couldn't believe that he had been such a fool as to waste three years before coming back after her. Well, he figured, he certainly wouldn't make *that* mistake again.

It had just occurred to him, too, in hearing Eula Mae's muttered agreement to his statement, the most nefarious part of the plan. "He figured that marrying you'd be the easiest way to get his hands on the ranch, didn't he?" Ramsey asked in barely controlled anger.

Eula Mae nodded. Her face flamed pink.

"Makes sense," Ramsey said tightly, feeling the anger grow. "Not only does he get the Big Horizon, he also gets the most beautiful woman in all of Colorado Territory, to boot." He was becoming enraged.

Eula Mae flushed again, but this time with pride that Ramsey would say such a thing.

Miss Eula Mae McFarrin was a smart young woman, and she had no delusions. She knew she was a fine-looking woman, a more than decent catch for any man. But with her streak of stubbornness and the smidgen of mischievousness, she had scared many men off. Except for Buck Ramsey—and Colin Weymouth. The former's attentions she had wanted all along. The latter's she didn't want at all in the beginning; she wanted them even less now. In addition, it reaffirmed Ramsey's feelings for her when he said such things aloud.

"Got good eyesight, well's good sense," Maybelle said with a low chuckle. She paused, then said quietly, "Now, girl, before you go gettin' all moon-eyed 'cause this here young man's nigh onto pledged his troth to you, best go fill our cups again."

Eula Mae grinned as she stood. Old Granny Maybelle certainly had a knack of bringing her back to earth on those occasions she needed it. "Yes'm." She did as she was told.

The action also gave Ramsey a little time to think some more, trying to sort things out. He still wasn't sure of what to do, but he figured that now he knew what was going on, he'd come up with a plan sooner or later. He sat back down and took a sip of the hot, black coffee.

"Don't you take sugar?" Eula Mae asked.

Ramsey smiled. "You spend as much time on the trail as I have, you sort of grow out of usin' sugar. I'd be obliged for some now, though." He shoved his cup toward Eula Mae.

Eula Mae grinned. She felt almost giddy as she spooned sugar into Ramsey's cup. She had not known she would feel so good serving Buck Ramsey. She decided she liked it; she wouldn't with anyone else, but she did with Buck.

Ramsey looked from one woman to the other. He imagined that Maybelle must have looked quite a bit like Eula Mae when she was that young. She still retained a certain beauty, disguised though it was by the wrinkles and years and travails.

"It's been hard on y'all lately, ain't it?" he asked suddenly.

Both nodded.

"Colin's made it tough for everyone at the ranch," Eula Mae said quietly. "It ain't anything he's done, really, since he's never tried to harm any of us, but . . . well, I don't know." She paused to draw in a raggedy breath. "He's . . . he always seems threatening. With all the money and connections Colin's got, he could do us some real harm, maybe." She paused. "He's been gettin' angrier the past couple of days, too."

"Why? You think he'd be more relaxed. As far as he knows, I'm out of the way, givin' him a clear chance to come after you—one way or the other."

Eula Mae nodded. "We expected that, too. But I—we—think he's bein' pressured by the railroad."

"How?"

"I'm not sure, Buck," Eula Mae said with a shrug. "But I think it's because . . . well, we heard that the railroad folks'll only bring the railroad through this area if Colin gets his hands on the Big Horizon."

Ramsey nodded. He thought he understood. Any railroad was a profit-making proposition. No profit could be made with delay. Ramsey figured the Midland Central officials must be real close to having to plan their line through this part of the territory. They would need to know about the ranch one way or the other. Most likely, they had been leaning on Weymouth hard, possibly even threatening him.

"I'm scared, Buck," Eula Mae said. She could hardly suppress a shudder. "Colin's been tryin' to bend us to his will by usin' threats and such. So far, Pa's held him off, but I'm real afraid he's going to . . . Well, I'm afraid he'll commence usin' violence soon to get his way."

"Over my dead body," Ramsey hissed.

Maybelle laughed in relief. She had known all along she could count on Buck Ramsey.

Ramsey was startled by the sound, but then he nodded, a tight, vicious grin on his face.

Maybelle patted her white hair, some of which was straying out of the bun in which she almost always wore it. "And," she said suddenly, "lest you ain't mad enough at all these goin's on, me and Eula found out that your arrest was set up by Weymouth, that snip of a girl and her curmudgeon father. We think, but ain't sure, that the sheriff was mixed up in it, too. Or at least knew about it."

Ramsey was bothered by that, but not too much. It did serve to feed his anger more than a little, though.

"Worse," Eula Mae added, "we also found out that Colin hired the men who attacked you that time a few days before that incident when you were arrested."

Ramsey was enraged. The jail time was something he could live with. It had only been a couple of days. Even the flight from the posse, and the dangers he had been forced to face afterward, were something he could handle. But in the assault at least two men had died. Others, including innocents, could have fallen.

He nodded in determination. *Yes*, he thought, *Mr. Colin Weymouth has a heap to pay for.*

CHAPTER

★ 15 ★

"We've got to figure out what to do about all this," Ramsey said, beginning to pace once more.

He was not used to this. Almost always, in situations like this, he had been with Matt or Kyle, or both. He generally would defer to them because of their age and experience. But now it was all up to him, and he was not sure he liked the responsibility. However, he had no choice. It was all up to him.

"I have faith in you, Buck," Eula Mae said softly. She reddened in embarrassment, but no one made light of her. "You'll figure out what to do. I know you will."

"For once," Maybelle said with a chuckle, "I have to agree with my granddaughter."

Ramsey looked stricken. The only thing he could think to do was to head out and kill Colin Weymouth. He knew if he did that, though, he would be hunted down and hanged.

"Don't fret over it now, Buck," Maybelle offered, seeing the look on his face. "I know you'll think of somethin'. You'll have to digest all what you've learned here today; run it around in your mind before you can figure out what's best to do."

Ramsey nodded reluctantly. He knew she was right, but his impatience called for him to do something—anything—now. He wanted to go out and hit or smash or shoot something or someone. But all that was infinitely impractical.

"We've got to go now, Buck," Maybelle added. "We've been out longer than usual. Somebody might get suspicious." Seeing the longing with which Ramsey looked at Eula Mae, Maybelle said, "Now, listen, Buck, y'all come on to the ranch house tonight. You can stay there. We've got places where you won't be seen.

Once we're all together, we can figure out what to do."

Ramsey nodded at first, but then he shook his head. "No, Miz Maybelle," he said thoughtfully. "I'll come for some supplies." He paused, thinking. "But I won't stay."

"Why?" Eula Mae asked. She felt crushed that he would not want to be near her. Perhaps, she worried, he didn't love her anymore. He had had his way with her, and with her full consent. Maybe he was going to discard her now.

"I'll feel more comfortable out here in the open where I can move," he said slowly, not really seeing Eula Mae's pain and worry. "Less chance of gettin' trapped." He smiled at Eula Mae. "It'll be hell stayin' away from you any longer," he added fervently.

Relief washed over Eula Mae like water over a falls.

"All right," Maybelle said. She stood, yawning. "Till tonight then."

"No, not tonight." He thought again, then nodded. "Tomorrow night maybe. Or the next." He grinned. "We've got to be careful. You never know, Sheriff Burleson might have the house and the area around it watched."

Seeing the look of worry that dulled Eula Mae's beauty only fractionally, he added, "I don't really expect him to do that, mind you. But in such matters, it always pays to be extra careful."

The two women nodded. Eula Mae stood and began gathering up the cups and such that had been dirtied. She dumped them in a small wood tub that Ramsey had filled with water that morning.

While Eula Mae did that, Maybelle said, "It's a good thing you're a cautious man, Buck."

"Oh?" He looked at her with a question in his eyes.

"We've heard that Weymouth is beginnin' to import some gunmen to put down any resistance that might arise. Or to intimidate my son-in-law. He'll try to do the same with you—if he finds out you're still in these parts."

Ramsey nodded. He escorted the two women outside and helped them onto the carriage. Eula Mae looked glum. Ramsey kissed her long and lovingly, despite Maybelle sitting right alongside the girl.

Maybelle stared off into space, a small, secret smile on her lips. Caleb would have done the same thing; he had, in fact, more than once, shocking friends and neighbors.

"We'll be together again soon, Eula," Ramsey said with quiet determination.

She looked at him, eagerness—and some sadness—in her bright blue eyes.

"And," he added, hoping that Maybelle would not hear—or say anything if she did hear—"once we get all this cleared up, there won't be no separatin' us." His heart was thumping. Never in the midst of all his battles had his heart beat like this.

The look on her face made the fear in his heart fade like fog under the assault of the summer sun. He stepped back, happier than he had ever been. He watched a little sadly as Maybelle cracked the whip and the big buttermilk horse trotted away. The carriage rattled behind, bouncing on the rough ground.

When the carriage was out of sight, Ramsey turned and strolled into the sod shack. Trying to keep his mind off his growing loneliness, he brought Biscuit outside and tied him to a bush. He went back inside and began preparing supper for himself. It helped keep his mind occupied only a little.

After he ate, he brought the horse back inside and then sat down at the table, a cup of coffee at his side. He began cleaning, oiling, and reloading his weapons. While he did, he couldn't help but run the problem he faced through his mind.

It was, he had to admit, an intriguing predicament. He wished that either Kyle or Matt—or, preferably, both—were here with him. Among the three of them, they would be able to plot a course of action. And if they couldn't, there was nothing the three couldn't confront head-on.

He knew, however, that he had to start leaning on himself. Not that there was anything wrong in counting on family. Even Kyle, the most fractious and independent of the Ramsey brothers, needed the family's help of a time. Not that Kyle would *ask* for help. But he sure as hell didn't turn it down when it was offered.

Buck might wish all he wanted that his brothers were there. But they weren't, and he would have to make do by himself. And that, he decided, was not such a bad thing after all. He was young, strong, resourceful. He had had good training in survival and strategy from Matt and Kyle. He could handle himself well in any situation.

That still did not tell him what he had to do to clear this situation up. But he forced it away from his mind. The answer would come when it was needed.

For now he preferred thinking of Eula Mae. The thoughts were pleasurable, though perhaps more exciting than was good for him.

Still, the thoughts of her . . . and him . . . together were far, far
better than thoughts of facing Colin Weymouth in a fist fight or
something possibly worse.

His loneliness and worry were gone by the time he crawled into
the blankets on the one cot. He smiled when he thought back about
six hours and what had occurred in this cot. He fell asleep with the
smile still on his face and pleasurable thoughts still in his mind.

He spent the next day tending to Biscuit, refilling the wood
box and making a few minor though much needed repairs to the
soddy.

In the early afternoon, despite the scorching heat that had risen
again after a few days of some respite, he saddled Biscuit and rode
in wide circles around the soddy. Each circle was a little farther
out than the next. He was looking for nothing in particular, just
wanting to check his surroundings.

He saw little sign of anything, other than some deer and a
buffalo or two. After a couple of hours he headed toward the
soddy, working in circles that slowly narrowed. Several times he
splashed across Horse Creek. He saw no signs of anyone having
come this way, other than himself, and the carriage used by Eula
Mae and Maybelle.

When dark came Ramsey was fairly satisfied that he was safe
here. He expected it to remain that way. He still had every
intention of staying here, riding down to the ranch house only
every couple of days for supplies. He didn't figure that it would
take too long to clear up this mess. He still was not sure how he
would do it, but once he began to move, he didn't figure it would
take long.

Somehow, he felt that deep in his mind, he was working on
the problem of what to do. He went about making his supper,
not letting himself dwell on the problem. He was confident now
that it would be worked out in due time.

After his supper of beans, salted beef, and coffee, he repaired
a tear in his saddle scabbard. Finished, he stood and stretched. He
kicked off his boots and stripped down to his longjohns. Crawling
into the covers on the cot, he was asleep quickly.

Biscuit's urgent nickering woke him sometime in the night.
Ramsey lay there for a bit, trying to discern just what was bothering
the horse. A soft, almost undiscernible sound came to him, and
Ramsey rolled out of the cot. He reached for his Colt.

In his longhandles, with his pistol in hand, Ramsey moved
silently around the furniture until he was standing next to Biscuit.

He patted the horse's muzzle with his left hand. "Good boy," he whispered.

He stood there for some minutes, senses heightened. He knew something was out there. Biscuit was too well trained to nicker in that particular way for no good reason. Ramsey only wished he knew what—or who—was out there.

He thought he heard another sound outside, and he slipped away from the horse's side toward the window at back. He edged up toward the window along the wall and peered out.

Pale silver light coated the almost flat, grassy land, lending it an eerie look and feel. Ramsey stood there, eyes roving over the desolate landscape, looking for any sign of life. Other than the grass ruffling in the breeze, there was nothing to be seen.

Then he spotted something slinking along the ground maybe twenty yards from the cabin. It was far too big to be a snake. It took some moments to discern what it actually was, what with the light being so low and odd.

The figure eventually revealed itself to be an Indian. Ramsey wasn't sure, but he could swear it was one of the Cheyennes he had faced down on the island only three weeks before.

"Damn," he said only in his head. He could hardly believe it. Then he began to worry. If this one Cheyenne was here, others might also be. Even more unbelievable was the thought that their courses might have crossed again.

Worried that other warriors might be closing in on the shack, he moved swiftly and surely across the dark room to the front window. It took several moments to pick out the creeping form. Ramsey hurriedly swept to the other two walls. Sure enough, there was an Indian inching up on each side of the soddy.

He wondered what to do. He knew that the Cheyennes had seen the last of their good days, that these warriors were among the last of their kind. He had no desire to kill them, adding to the bloodbath they and their people had already faced. On the other hand, he was plumb sick and tired of armed folks following him, trying to shoot him or stab him or in some other way do him harm.

He whirled, raced across the inky room and grabbed his holster. He jammed the Colt into it and buckled it on. Then he stuffed his feet into his boots. He knew he made a ludicrous sight, but he didn't much give a damn. This was war.

Ramsey grabbed his Winchester and headed toward the front window. That Cheyenne had been closest to the soddy, and Ramsey figured he better handle that one first.

He was glad, as he worked the Winchester's lever, that he had been taught to take such good care of his weapons. The rifle's action moved smoothly, making only the barest of clicking sounds as the cartridge slid into the chamber and the hammer was forced back until it was cocked. Ramsey hoped that with the thick sod walls the warrior would not have heard it.

CHAPTER

★ 16 ★

Ramsey stopped at the side of the front window and scanned the silvery landscape. He knew where he had seen the Cheyenne warrior before, but that was no guarantee he would still be in the same general area.

He was right in thinking that. Not only had the Cheyenne moved closer to the soddy, he had angled a little to the east, presumably, Ramsey thought, to throw off any possible detection.

Ramsey managed to pick him out of the shadows after a few moments. Ramsey eased the rifle up.

The Cheyenne was only about ten yards away. The pistol might be better for the shot, but Ramsey was more comfortable using the Winchester. He took a deep breath, let it out slowly. Halfway out, he stopped. Then he fired.

The Cheyenne made no sound as he died in the grass. The other three yelled and charged.

Ramsey spun, sliding his back against the front wall to the corner. He darted swiftly to the hole in the side wall. He knelt there in front of the hole, rifle cocked. A Cheyenne was sticking his head through the wall, just about to burst into the room. Ramsey recognized the hawklike face and broad, flabby chest of the warrior he had shot during the fight on the island in the Arkansas. He fired the rifle. The blast was shockingly loud and powerful in the relatively confined space. The Cheyenne was blown backward outside.

Ramsey didn't wait around to see it, though. When a bullet thudded into the wall inches from his head, he whirled and dived toward his cot. He bounced and rolled awkwardly, crashing into the cot.

As he struggled to extricate himself from the tangle of cot and blankets, he pulled the Colt. He freed himself just in time to get a shot off at a Cheyenne who was stalking him with a tomahawk in hand. He fired again as the Indian began to fall.

Ramsey stood up, thumbing back the hammer of the revolver. He pointed it at the side window, where a Cheyenne warrior was just climbing through.

"Stop," Ramsey ordered.

The Indian froze, half in, half out of the window.

"I've got no hankerin' to send you to the Happy Huntin' Grounds with your friends there, but you come in that goddamn window, and you'll join 'em sure as God made flowers."

The warrior still had not moved.

"You speak English, boy?" Ramsey asked. Exasperation began to grow. He really was tired of people trying to kill him.

The Indian still said nothing and had not moved.

Frustrated, Ramsey fired. The bullet chunked into the wall next to the window, not far from the warrior's head. "Answer me, goddamnit," Ramsey roared in anger.

"Some," the warrior said warily.

"Good," Ramsey said in more reasonable tones. "Now, what're you and your pals doin' here?"

"Lookin' for you."

"Why?"

"After fight along river, Black Weasel was angry. You killed his brother, Star Falling. And you killed Bull Walker. As war chief, that made Black Weasel look bad. He wanted revenge." He shrugged. He was cramped perched in the window as he was, but he would not let this white man see it.

"And you come lookin' for me?" Ramsey was still rather incredulous that they would do such a thing.

"Yes."

Ramsey shook his head. He realized that the warrior must be quite uncomfortable, so he waved the pistol. "Come on in all the way. But go easy."

The warrior clambered inside and leaned back against the wall next to the window.

"Ain't you lost enough of your people over the years to want to continue such foolishness?" Ramsey asked, a note of sadness in his voice.

The Cheyenne remained stony-faced.

"You leave the reservation to make war on folks?"

The warrior looked like he was going to remain adamantly mum. But when Ramsey thumbed back the Colt's hammer, the warrior said, "Yes." There was an infinite sorrow in his dark, forbidding eyes. "The old days are gone. But Black Weasel, Star Falling, Buffalo Back, Bull Walker, He Dog, and me decided to die like warriors in the old times." He shrugged. The feeling of pride he had been trying to develop struggled for a foothold. "Now I'm the only one left."

"What's your name, boy?"

"Iron Shield."

"There's been too much killin' between our peoples, Iron Shield," Ramsey said somberly. "I know your people've suffered a heap over the years. Ain't nothin' either one of us can do about that now. But we don't have to try killin' each other no more."

The Cheyenne eyed him cautiously. "What're you sayin'?" he asked flatly.

"I'm sayin' we can both walk away from this encounter with our lives. Or I can walk away from it by myself."

"You think you could kill me?" the Cheyenne asked haughtily. He drew himself up straight.

"What do you think?" Ramsey's Colt had never wavered from the warrior's chest.

Iron Shield blinked and nodded. "What do we do?"

"That's up to you."

"You got the gun."

Ramsey nodded. "Yep. But the choice is yours. If you choose to, you can walk away from here. You can take your friends back to your people and give 'em what honors you think they deserve and such."

"What do you want from me?" Iron Shield asked. He was suspicious, but hope burned inside him.

"Your word that you'll go back to your people, that you won't go out killin' no more. Your word that you won't come lookin' for me no more."

"You'd take my word on those things?" the Cheyenne asked with incredulity.

"Was you to give it honestly I would."

Iron Shield found that hard to believe. White-eyes had been lying to him all his life, and to his people since time began, he supposed. The old ones often talked of the forked tongue of the white-eyes. But for some reason he saw truth in the young white man's eyes, and he heard it in the man's voice. He decided he could do worse than to at least partially trust this hard-eyed young man.

"I will do as you say," Iron Shield said solemnly.

Ramsey nodded and uncocked the Colt. He knew he was taking a great risk, but he had to show some faith in this Indian. The warrior had given his word, as had Ramsey. They each had to trust the other. He slid the pistol into the holster.

"You got horses?"

"Yes." He jerked his head. "Across the stream."

Ramsey nodded again. "Go and fetch 'em."

Iron Shield stood there for a moment, staring at Ramsey. Each man was still wondering whether he could trust the other, whether the other would turn against him at any moment. Iron Shield finally shrugged. He turned and marched silently to the door and out.

When the Cheyenne was outside, Ramsey moved to the window and watched. After Iron Shield disappeared into the brush, Ramsey walked back and righted his cot. Keeping his Winchester nearby, he quickly unbuckled his gunbelt, put on pants and shirt and then put his gunbelt back on. He swiftly replaced the spent shells in the Colt and Winchester before heading back to the window to watch.

He was beginning to suspect that Iron Shield wasn't coming back when the Indian emerged from the brush leading four ponies. Leaving his rifle inside, Ramsey went out. Iron Shield paused in midstep, half expecting an attack. But Ramsey headed toward the nearest body. He stopped and waited.

When Iron Shield stopped there, too, Ramsey asked, "You want help gettin' your friends on the horses?"

The Cheyenne stared at the Texan a moment. Then he nodded once, sharply.

As the two placed the dead warrior over the horse as gently as they could, Ramsey asked, "You ain't mad at me for killin' your friends?" He wasn't afraid, but he did not want this feud to continue. If it had to go on, and end in another death, best to get it over with now.

"I ain't pleased," Iron Shield allowed as he tied the body down with horsehair rope. "But they all died as warriors. And you fought honorably. I—they—could ask no more." He paused. "I won't come seekin' revenge against you."

Ramsey looked at him for a few moments. He believed the warrior. He nodded.

It did not take long to gather up the two other bodies and lash them down across the backs of ponies. It was a sad and sobering job, but the two men did it with a minimum of fuss.

When it was done, Ramsey and Iron Shield stood for a little. Each was immersed in his own thoughts, and wondering what the other was thinking. Finally Iron Shield said, "You're not like other white-eyes."

Ramsey shrugged. He was proud and embarrassed at the same time. "Just doin' what's right is all," he offered.

"If there were more white-eyes like you . . ." He could not finish the thought. It was too painful.

Ramsey nodded. He understood how Iron Shield felt. What he could not understand—never could—was how men could hate other men for no reason. Lord knew there were enough reasons to hate someone without having to conjure up others up out of thin air. He sighed. There was no changing human nature. Occasionally, at times like these, two people could find a meeting of the minds, even if they had started off trying to kill each other. It was a fleeting moment in time and usually could not be matched.

"Best be movin' on, Iron Shield."

The Cheyenne nodded. He wanted to shake this white-eyes' hand, but he thought that might be asking too much of the white man. He swept onto the pony's back in one smooth leap. Ramsey handed him the rope to the other horses. He nodded and kicked his pony. They moved off.

Ramsey watched for some time, though the Cheyenne had faded from view quickly in the darkness that signaled that dawn was not far off. Finally Ramsey turned and walked slowly back into the soddy. Still dressed, he lay on the cot and dozed.

The heat woke him. Grimacing at the lack of sleep, the bloodshed of the night before, and just a general unease, Ramsey wandered down to the spring. He stripped down and jumped in, shrugging off the apprehension. It was entirely possible that Iron Shield would return, but he could not live his life worrying about every little possibility. He had to trust in the Lord and in human nature at least once in a while.

The dip in the cool water was refreshing. He went back and made himself a hearty breakfast. Since his supplies were running low, he decided that he would head to the ranch house tonight. Besides, he missed Eula Mae.

Ramsey took a slow walk around the place. He found blood spots in several places, but they were the only signs that a violent and deadly battle had taken place there only hours before. With the first good rain, there would be no sign left at all.

He had a goodly portion of the day to get through yet, before he would leave for the ranch house. He spent it in more chores around the soddy. He figured if he was going to be holing up there for any amount of time, he might as well be as comfortable as he could get. Throwing himself into work, the time passed quickly. As the sun began to fade, he took another dip in the spring to wash away the sweat of his labors, as well as the dust from the cabin.

Feeling the eagerness grow, he hurriedly saddled Biscuit. He climbed on and rode slowly off. The sun was dying, casting oddly long shadows amid the fading red and gold. Half a mile off, Ramsey stopped. Turning in the saddle, he looked back, wondering if Iron Shield had made it safely back to his people. He hoped so.

He moved on again, thoughts of Iron Shield and the other Cheyennes fading as visions of Eula Mae grew in his mind. He moved Biscuit a little faster.

In an hour, with the sunlight gone and the moonlight just beginning to appear, he spotted the ranch house.

CHAPTER

★ 17 ★

Buck Ramsey had never been so surprised and flabbergasted in all his twenty years. He stood in the doorway leading to the parlor of Artemis McFarrin's house and just stared, unable to speak.

He had waited a bit after first seeing the house, until full darkness was covering him. Then he rode slowly toward it. He didn't see Colin Weymouth's horse tied up out front, so he figured it was safe to ride up to the house.

Clarissa opened the front door warily—one just didn't yank open the front door of the McFarrin place these days, not at night. The old black woman smiled. "Welcome, Mistah Ramsey," she said.

"Evenin', Clarissa. Is Miss Eula home?" He knew he didn't have to ask, but he was always as polite as he could be.

Before Clarissa could answer, though, Eula Mae flew down the short hallway, burst between the servant and the door, and yanked the door wide open. She almost knocked Ramsey over as she leapt into his arms.

He staggered back across the porch a few steps under the loving assault, as she covered his face with kisses.

"That's quite enough, young lady," Maybelle said. There was no anger there, just acknowledgment that enough time had been spent on such things and that there were more important things to be done. As well as acknowledging the lack of propriety, even though it was dark out and no one could see.

"Oh, Granny," Eula Mae complained in a mock whine. But she pulled herself reluctantly from Ramsey's arms.

"Evenin', Miz Maybelle," Ramsey said.

"Mr. Ramsey." The words were polite, but Ramsey sensed something more than a greeting behind the old woman's enigmatic smile.

Ramsey looked at Eula Mae again. He had missed her terribly, and was glad to be back in her presence again. But she, too, was grinning more than he thought she might be. It confused him some.

"Well, girl, invite the poor man in," Maybelle said. She rolled her eyes, but her grin widened.

"Oh," Eula Mae squeaked. "Of course. Come on in, Buck. Where're my manners?"

She seemed more flustered than was called for, and that also made Ramsey wonder. Something must be up, Ramsey thought. Since they were not worried, Ramsey figured that whatever it was could not be threatening. Indeed, the two women seemed to be in far better spirits than they had been since Ramsey had arrived at the Big Horizon three weeks ago.

Eula Mae slipped her right arm through Ramsey's left, and they slowly followed Maybelle into the house. Ramsey pushed the big door shut behind them.

Maybelle stopped long enough to say to Clarissa, "Have Billy tend to Mr. Ramsey's horse. I want him in the barn, out of sight."

"Yes'm. What about Mistah Weymouth?"

Anger flashed across Maybelle's face. "I've told him not to come by. If he shows his face, you tell him Miss Eula ain't to be disturbed. He gives you a hard time, you come fetch me."

"Yes'm."

Clarissa headed for the front door, while the other three continued their procession down the hallway.

Ramsey could feel excitement growing inside Eula Mae. Somehow, her blood seemed to be singing in her veins, transmitted through her hand to his arm.

Maybelle entered the parlor and stepped aside. Ramsey allowed Eula Mae in, and she moved to the other side of the doorway, as Ramsey walked inside. And he stopped, flabbergasted. Emotions roared through him, and he found himself unable to speak.

"This any way to greet your old brothers, Buck?" Matt asked. He and Kyle stood there grinning at Buck.

"Maybe he don't want to see us, Matt," Kyle said, grin widening.

"I expect," Matt responded. "Probably figures that two handsome fellers like us come on in here, we'll just take his sweetheart away from him without even tryin'." He winked at Eula Mae.

The young woman blushed, but grinned widely, excitement running rampant inside her.

"How . . . ? Where . . . ? How . . . ?" Buck stammered.

He stopped and took a deep breath. He finally managed to collect his wits. He whooped. "Lord, it's good to see you two big galoots," he said happily. He stepped up and gave each big brother a quick, hard hug of welcome.

He stepped back a couple of paces and looked the two over. It had not been too long since he had seen Kyle, but it had been some months since he and Matt had spent any time together. Both brothers looked the same, though.

All three Ramseys were big men, broad-shouldered and strong. Buck and Kyle were the closest in looks. They had fair skin, deep blue eyes, and straw-colored hair. Only the age showing on Kyle's more weather-beaten face, and his stump of a left arm, set him apart from his youngest brother.

Where Buck and Kyle were fair, Matt was dark. He had dark, gleaming brown eyes and a shock of black hair. His skin tone was somewhat darker, too. It gave him a dangerous, deadly look. Many people shied away from him because of that. A few saw it as a reason to challenge him. Other folks, seeing that look, tended to turn toward Kyle or Buck as easier marks, usually to their regret.

"What in hell are you two doin' here?" Buck asked.

"Come to steal your woman," Matt said with a grin. "Told you that already."

"Well, I ain't going to be stole by neither of you," Eula Mae said firmly, though she was still grinning. She had decided to try to get in on the fun. She moved up and slipped her arm through Buck's. "So's you might's well tell him the real reason."

"You sure you want a woman feisty as that one, Buck?" Kyle asked with a laugh. "You'll get no peace and quiet from her, I'd think."

"She'll do," Buck offered. Hoping he would not hurt her feelings, and hoping that she would know he was joshing, he added, "But it might take some time to break her." He grinned at her, trying to let her know it was a joke. "But good fillies always do."

Eula Mae looked shocked for a moment. But when she looked at Buck's face, she felt relief. She knew he was not serious, and she relaxed. But she couldn't resist saying *sotto voce*, "Might take longer'n you think."

Matt laughed. "I think you're gonna have your hands full there, Buck." He grew serious. "You've picked a fine young lady there, boy."

Kyle nodded in agreement.

"I know," Buck said proudly. "Now, tell me, what're you two doin' here?"

"Well," Matt started.

"Sit, y'all," Maybelle said jovially. "Granddaughter, drinks for the men. What kind of hostess are you?"

"A poor one, it seems," Eula Mae said, abashed. She had been so excited by the reunion, that she had forgotten her manners and duties.

She hurriedly filled four glasses with fine bourbon. While she did so, the men sat. Then Eula Mae gave each man a drink. She handed the fourth glass to Maybelle. The old lady smiled as she took the drink and sipped at it.

"All right, boys, 'fess up," Buck said after tasting the smooth bourbon.

"I think," Eula Mae said, suddenly shy, "that I'd better explain it."

Ramsey looked at the young woman in surprise. She shyly smiled back. She licked her lips, then started. "The trouble with Colin didn't just crop up since you've been here," she said. "It started five, six months ago, when he first showed up." She sighed. "Anyway, a couple months ago, I was gettin' worried about it all, so I decided to write to you."

"I was up by Kyle," Buck said.

"I know that. Now. But how could I know that then?" She looked bitter. "I had waited almost three years for you to come callin' on me. I really thought that you'd never be back, that you'd found someone else and didn't even think of me no more." Her voice contained hurt, anger.

"I got caught up in things at first," Buck said quietly. "After we parted down in Justice, I had Matt to worry about. Then one thing after another come up." He looked sad, and ashamed. "By then, more than a year had passed. I figured for sure that by then some new beau would've come along and taken you away."

"Why?" Eula Mae asked. The thought had crossed her mind, but she had always held out the hope that Buck would come back for her.

"A woman's beautiful as you . . ." He couldn't finish it.

She did it for him, " . . . don't always meet a man like you."
She smiled softly.

"I'm glad you waited," he said, embarrassed as out of the corner
of his eyes he caught his two brothers grinning widely at him.

Eula Mae smiled in delight. "Well, I didn't know any of that
then, of course. All I knew was that you were the only one I could
think of to maybe help us—if you were willin'. So I wrote to you.
I didn't say much about the trouble in the letter—only that the
family was havin' some difficulty and that I'd really be obliged
for your help, could you see your way clear to providin' it."

"I would've come directly, had I been home to get the letter."

"I know," Eula Mae said quietly. She smiled again. All those
fears of him not caring about her had long since faded. "So, when
you showed up on the doorstep a couple weeks ago, I just figured
it was because of my letter. That's why I didn't question why
you had come here. I knew that you'd give me all the help I
needed."

What Eula Mae had just told him cleared up a number of things
for Buck. It didn't, however, clear up how his brothers had come
to be at the Big Horizon Ranch. He mentioned that.

"Kyle had come out to help me in some business over in West
Texas," Matt explained. "I'd been out scoutin' out some new
country for catchin' mustangs when I got caught up in a spot
of trouble." He shrugged. Such things happened so often to all
the Ramseys that details were hardly worth bringing up anymore.
"When we got back to Amos's, we found Miss Eula's letter to
you." He grinned. "Just on the chance it was somethin' other than
a love letter, we opened it."

"And I'm glad you did," Eula said.

"Yes'm." He grinned at Buck. "Once we saw she was in
trouble—and I knew what she'd meant to you once, boy—me
and Kyle headed here hell for leather." He paused. "And here
we are."

Buck grinned. He was greatly relieved that he would not have
to face this trouble alone. "I think I feel the same way as Eula
does," he said. "Glad you read that letter, and mighty glad you've
shown up."

"We was hopin' it was a love letter, though," Kyle threw in,
grinning. "Would've been a heap more interestin'."

They all enjoyed a laugh. Feeling almost giddy, Eula Mae
went around and filled the men's glasses. She filled her grandmother's, too.

Kyle set his glass down on a table. He rolled and lit a cigarette. Eula Mae offered Matt a cigar. He took it with a nod of thanks.

"So," Matt said when everyone was settled in, "what's this big problem that's got y'all caught up?"

Buck, Maybelle and Eula Mae explained it rather quickly. Matt and Kyle sat nodding in understanding.

Buck, watching his two brothers, could see the wheels turning in their minds as they processed the information. They were already formulating plans. He wished he possessed that faculty, but he didn't and probably never would.

"So?" Buck asked when the story had unfolded. "What're we gonna do, brothers?"

"Set things to right," Matt said with determination.

"Hell, I've known that all along," Buck snorted. "What I want to know, is how?"

"Let's sleep on it," Matt said. "We'll decide in the mornin'."

"I wasn't plannin' to stay here at the ranch," Buck said.

"Plans change," Kyle said mildly.

"Reckon they do." Buck grinned. He was feeling very good now. Nothing could stop the Ramseys when they put their minds to setting something to rights. It would all work out. He lifted his glass in salute. Then he wondered where McFarrin was. It seemed odd that the rancher would not be here at such a time.

CHAPTER

★18★

Matt and Kyle Ramsey were less than impressed with Dirt Creek when they rode into town the next morning. They had left Buck back at the ranch house, having decided that it would be best if the youngest Ramsey brother was not seen in public just yet.

Buck had protested, wanting to get in on the action as soon as possible, but his brothers and Eula Mae convinced him it would be in his—and the McFarrins'—best interests if he stayed at the ranch. That would not only keep him out of general sight; it also would offer the McFarrins some protection should Weymouth think to cause trouble. Of even if he should show up.

Buck reluctantly agreed finally, but he was still not happy with it. Part of the reason he was less than happy was that he liked action and he was afraid he would miss out on some by staying at the ranch. Another big reason was that while he wanted very much to be with Eula Mae, he was not certain, even now, that McFarrin would let the two lovebirds be alone together for more than a few moments. That was a bittersweet agony—being so close to Eula Mae but being unable to touch her, or even really talk privately with her.

He had finally gotten around to asking where McFarrin was last night. Eula had looked angry, and Maybelle said with a scowl, "Seems like he don't think none of this is right somehow."

"Why?" Buck asked, surprised.

"Who knows," Maybelle said with a shrug.

That all bothered Buck. He had thought McFarrin had come to grips with the thought of his courting Eula Mae by now, and with the thought that some killing might take place to straighten all this mess out. The more he thought about it, the angrier he got. "Where is he?" Buck growled.

"What're you gonna do?" Eula Mae countered, alarmed.

"Settle it."

Maybelle grinned. "In his den."

Buck nodded and rose. As he headed for the door, he smiled tightly at Eula Mae and said quietly, "Don't worry."

He found McFarrin at his desk in the den.

McFarrin did not look happy with Buck's sudden presence. "Somethin' I can do for you, Buck?" he asked with forced politeness.

"Tell me just what the hell's stuck in your craw."

"Ain't a thing stuck in my craw, Buck," McFarrin said blandly.

Buck's anger flared. "Bullshit," he snapped. He had been standing right in front of the desk. Now he slapped his palms on its surface and leaned forward, thrusting his face at McFarrin. "Now, you listen to me, Artemis," Buck hissed. "I aim to marry Miss Eula—as soon as we get the mess around here cleaned up."

"I'm obliged for your help, Buck. Yours and your brothers'. I really am." McFarrin looked pained. "I've got nothing against you. Hell, you've done plenty to help me and my family. And for that, I'll always be in your debt." He tried to sound humble.

"But?" Buck asked, knowing it was coming. He pushed off his hands, straightening. Then he sat.

"But, well, mainly I'm concerned for my daughter's future. Can you see that?" His eyes pleaded for understanding.

"I suppose," Buck said softly. "But there ain't gonna be no one care for Eula better'n me, Mr. McFarrin."

"I don't doubt your sincerity, Buck. But what're your prospects?" He leaned forward, resting his elbows on the desk. "You've got no trade except handlin' a gun. What'll you do? How'll you support a wife? And," he added with a small smile, "maybe some young 'uns?"

"I'll think of something." It was lame, and even Buck knew it.

"I can't be sure of that."

Silence grew and expanded. Finally Buck said, "Us fightin' about all this ain't gonna accomplish a damn thing, when we got Weymouth and all his schemin' to concern us. Me and my brothers can take care of it. But we'll need your help." He paused. "After that, we can worry about me and Eula. Till then, though, I'd be obliged if you was to give me—us—a chance."

"Listen to him, Father," Eula Mae said. She walked into the room, stopping by Buck's chair. She rested a hand on one of his shoulders.

"How long were you listening, Daughter?" McFarrin asked. He looked almost haunted.

"Long enough." She bit her lower lip. Then she went behind the desk, stopping behind her father. She stroked his hair softly. "Things've been hard on all of us, Father," he said quietly. "Most of all you." She smiled at Buck. "He really don't have all that much against us, Buck. Mostly it's the trouble with Colin. It's preyin' on his mind. Ain't that right, Father?"

McFarrin reached up and patted one of Eula Mae's hands. "I was tryin' to keep it from you and Mother Sweet as much as possible," he said. "I didn't want to worry you."

"We ain't as dumb as you might think. Nor as scaredy."

"I know." McFarrin sounded weary.

"Well, Mr. McFarrin," Buck boasted, "you can put your mind at ease. With me, Matt, and Kyle, Weymouth doesn't stand a chance."

McFarrin sat quietly. Then he nodded.

In the morning, Buck was still not sure how McFarrin felt. So it was with split feelings that he watched his two big brothers head slowly down the trail toward Dirt Creek.

When Matt and Kyle rode into the town, they caught some attention. It wasn't often that two big men, well-armed and hard-eyed rode into Dirt Creek. It also helped to attract attention that one of the men had only one arm and the other was riding a magnificent, pitch black prairie mustang. People stopped and stared at the two riders.

The Ramseys were aware of the inspection they were undergoing, but they ignored it. They stopped and dismounted at The Ranchman, the fanciest saloon in town. It sat off the main section of town, sort of by itself. Such a location gave the place a special, regal look, setting it apart from the rest of the town. The saloon had been built by and for local ranch owners, and they were the ones who populated it. Cowboys could neither afford such a place nor enjoy its aura of richness.

McFarrin had told the Ramseys about The Ranchman. Buck had seen the place, but since it had no sign or anything, he had never stopped by. He had wondered what the fancy brick building was. Somehow, though, he had been too occupied to ask anyone about it.

The two brothers realized as soon as McFarrin told them about it that it might be the best place to find information about a man like Colin Weymouth. They might not learn anything, but it wouldn't hurt to try it first.

With a last look around, Matt and Kyle stepped inside. They were impressed by the saloon's rich wood tones and its aura of luxury. An armed man moved in front of them. "I believe you've come into the wrong place, gentlemen," the man said.

The Ramseys looked at the man blandly for a moment. He was as tall as they, but heavier than either, making him a very large man, indeed. He wore a shoulder rig with two Smith & Wesson revolvers.

"This is The Ranchman, ain't it?" Kyle said.

"Yes, sir."

"Then we're in the right place. Now step out of the way."

"This is for ranch owners only, boys," the man said evenly but with a hint of steel in his voice.

"We are ranch owners, boy," Kyle said jovially. "Own us a little spread—the Four Sevens—down in Texas. Ain't much, mind you. A little less'n a quarter of a million acres. But it's all ours." He smiled.

The man still looked skeptical.

"What's your name?" Matt asked.

"Wendall Fairweather."

"Look, Wendall," Kyle said evenly, as if confiding in the man, "we know our spread ain't much. But it's comin' along. Still, we're lookin' for a new place. We come up this way to see what we could buy in the way of a ranch."

"Why here in Dirt Creek?" Fairweather asked, still unconvinced.

"Main reason is we heard the railroad is plannin' to come on through here. That right?"

Fairweather's eyes brightened. "Yes, sir. The Midland Central is going to run a line right smack dab through town. It'll do a world of good for everybody."

"That's what we wanted to hear, Wendall," Kyle said enthusiastically. "Now, how's about you let us in here? We got a heap of dry that could use cuttin'."

Fairweather thought a moment, then nodded. "It's all right by me." He looked just a little rueful. "But I'll have to check with the head man. I figure he won't say no, considerin' you're here to buy some ranch land."

"About that," Kyle said in confidence, "we'd be obliged if you wasn't to say anything."

"Why?" Fairweather asked, suspicions aroused anew.

Kyle looked around to make sure no one was listening. "Word gets out we're here to buy land, folks're likely to jack the price up to stiff us." He winked. "Know what I mean?"

Fairweather nodded. "Yes, sir. I sure do." He smiled, honored to be sharing this little secret. "If you'll wait a moment, I'll speak to the ramrod." He started away, stopped, and turned back. "Who shall I say you are?"

"Graham," Kyle said. "He's Matthew; I'm Kyle."

The Ramseys nodded and waited patiently. "Good thinkin', Kyle," Matt said with a grin. "You concocted a real good story this time."

"That's 'cause I'm smarter'n you," Kyle said modestly. He grinned, too.

Before Matt could retort, Fairweather returned. "Welcome to The Ranchman, gentlemen. Mr. Weymouth, one of the principal benefactors of this establishment, says you're welcome at his table."

"Reckon that wouldn't put me out none," Matt said. "Kyle?"

The straw-haired brother shrugged.

"Fine. This way." He stepped off, with the Ramseys behind him. He stopped at a table.

Weymouth stood. "Colin Weymouth at your service, gentlemen." As he reached out to shake their hands, his eyes widened.

"These men are armed, Wendall," he said in some offense. He looked at the Ramseys. "I'm sorry, gentlemen, The Ranchman's rules prohibit the wearing of weapons." He shrugged in regret.

"A Texan don't give up his weapons for no man," Matt said. The words were said pleasantly enough, but there could be no mistaking the warning.

Kyle smiled. "And, I'd feel downright naked without my LeMat." He pointed to the stump of his left arm.

Weymouth thought for a moment, then nodded. "I believe we can break the rules this one time. You won't cause any trouble, though, will you?" He smiled, letting them know he did not believe such a thing but that he wanted to reassure the two other men at the table.

"We're peaceable men, Mr. Weymouth," Kyle said blandly.

As the brothers sat, Weymouth was sure he could not believe Kyle's last statement. He sat, too. Drinks were ordered. The other two men left just before the drinks arrived.

Weymouth offered a salute and all three drank a little. Then Weymouth said, "We had a little trouble with a fellow Texan not long ago. A man named Ramsey. Buck Ramsey. You know him?"

"There's a heap of Ramseys in Texas," Matt said. "All over. Never heard of one named Buck, though."

Weymouth looked at him, as if doubting his words.

"Texas is a mighty big place, Mr. Weymouth," Kyle said soothingly. "Hell, we don't even know all the folks in Deaf Smith County, where our ranch is, let alone in all Texas."

Weymouth sat back, nodding. He was satisfied with the answers.

The Ramseys spent an hour sipping the quality whiskey and chatting. Both brothers were guarded in what they said, even though Weymouth probed as to their reasons for being in Dirt Creek.

Finally Matt stood up. "Obliged for your hospitality, Mr. Weymouth," he said. "But we got to be moseyin' on."

"My pleasure, Mr. Graham."

Kyle stood, too.

"You fellows have a place to stay?" Weymouth asked suspiciously. "My home is open to you."

"We've got a place," Matt said flatly.

"Where?"

"That's our business," Matt said with a slight edge to his voice.

Weymouth looked up at the two, eyes flickering from one Ramsey to the other. He did not believe them, though he wasn't sure why. But he was certain they were lying. And because of that he began to doubt everything they had said since they had walked into The Ranchman.

However, he realized they looked far too formidable to tangle with. He suspected that even Fairweather would have trouble handling just one of these two men. So he thought it unwise to mention his doubts to them. He would, however, do some checking up on them as soon as they were out the door.

He nodded, accepting their statement. Matt and Kyle marched out, glancing around casually as they did so. Outside, Matt said, "I figure Weymouth don't believe a damn thing we said, Kyle."

"I figure about the same." Kyle sighed and rubbed his wide jaw with his one big hand. "And I suspect we ain't gonna find out anything from anyone around here."

"Then we'll have to look elsewhere."

"Yep."

They mounted their horses and rode out of town, cutting across the prairie and rolling mounds to the east. At a crumbling, tilting old line shack a half mile out of town, they stopped. Neither needed to say anything. They had fought side by side for too long to need verbal communications in such things. They brought their mounts into the shack with them so the animals would not be seen. It made the crumbling little cabin crowded, but neither Ramsey noticed.

The two Ramseys did not have long to wait before they heard two horses coming hard. Both men smiled tightly. There was no humor in the grins, just the knowledge that they had been right.

The riders slowed as soon as they spotted the cabin, and they came on at a slow pace, trying to appear as if they were just out for a pleasure ride. The Ramseys were not fooled by it.

Matt pulled his big Colt .44, his brother drew out the odd-looking LeMat. They waited in the shadows inside the rickety shack, watching through the gaping maws of the old windows.

The riders pulled up to the shack. They sat for a minute. "Think they're inside?" one asked. He sounded nervous.

"Ain't seen any sign of 'em," the other said. He tried to brazen his way through.

"True enough. Let's ride on, then."

They spurred their horses and galloped off. Inside the shack, the Ramseys shoved past their own horses to the back and watched out of cracks in the boards. They stayed there for more than an hour, waiting.

Their patience was rewarded. The two riders came creeping on their bellies over the knoll behind the shack.

"Goddamn fools," Matt muttered. He hated to see such stupidity in people, especially when it usually was fatal. Kyle said nothing. He was more hardened to the idiocies of man.

"Let's take 'em outside," Matt said.

Kyle shrugged. He would not give the two creeping enemies a fair chance, like Matt was planning to do. It was not that he was any less confident of his abilities than his brother; it was just that he was not as willing to risk his neck with chance. Shooting the townsmen from the safety of the shack would be easiest, and safest. Out in the open, something could go wrong. A person could slip and fall; a pistol could misfire; an enemy's desperate shot could find a home. But risk was part of life.

They went out through the doorway, from which the door had long ago disappeared. Each slipped around one side, flat against the side wall. At the back corners they glanced out and saw the two other men a little closer. Matt nodded at his brother.

They stepped out into the open, slipping their pistols away, and walked toward the two men who were still crawling. Twenty feet away from the men, Matt said, "It's a heap easier to make progress by walkin', boys."

The two men looked up startled. They stood, brushing grass and dirt off themselves, trying to cover their embarrassment.

"What're you boys trailin' us for?" Matt asked harshly.

"We ain't trailin' you, mister," one said. He looked uneasy. "We heard there was an outlaw holed up in that shack and . . ."

"Bullshit," Matt snapped. "Now you got one chance and one chance only to save your miserable hides. You unbuckle them gunbelts and drop 'em. Then you walk back to Dirt Creek."

"Or?" the other man asked. He almost sneered. He fancied himself a gunslinger, and was certain he could take either one of these two big men. He figured that if his partner kept the other one occupied for a moment, he could take both of them.

Matt shrugged. "Even you can't be that stupid not to know the answer to that."

"Well," the would-be gunfighter said slowly, "then I reckon we'll just . . ." His hand darted for his pistol.

CHAPTER

★ 19 ★

It never cleared leather.

Kyle, who was nearest that man, had had his hand on the LeMat the whole time. It was but a moment before the pistol was out and Kyle fired. The blast of buckshot tore the man's stomach to pieces.

The other man tried for his pistol, too. Without hesitation, Matt drew his Colt and gunned the man down.

Silence descended. "Well, now what?" Kyle asked. He stuffed the barrel of the LeMat under his left armpit, broke the weapon, pulled out the old shell and inserted a new one. He snapped the pistol shut and dropped it into the cross-draw holster. By then, Matt had reloaded the Colt.

"Get the horses first," Matt said.

When they were back outside behind the shack with their horses, Matt said, "You stay here and keep an eye on things. I'm gonna go try'n find their horses." He leaped onto the black's back and galloped off.

He returned a few minutes later, leading two saddled horses. As he and Kyle were placing the bodies over the horses and tying them down, Kyle asked, "What do we do with them?"

Matt shrugged. "Got two choices, the way I see it. Send the horses headin' back to town; let those folks give 'em a decent burial. Or haul these horses a few miles out on the prairie and set 'em loose in another direction. Hope they can't find their way back here."

"We send 'em into town, folks're gonna connect us with it sure as shit."

"Yep."

"Then we ain't got but one choice."

"Yep." He tied the last knot tight. "Let's ride."

They set a fast, steady pace, heading west. A mile out, they curled southward and pushed a little harder. They eventually crossed the Arkansas River, which was cold and wide, but moving sluggishly. They followed the river a mile or so west and then southwest. Along a small creek, they stopped.

While Kyle kept a lookout, Matt quickly tied the horses carrying the bodies loosely to a bush. He figured the horses would work themselves free after a while. He jumped on his horse. The two men spun and raced off straight north. They took their time recrossing the Arkansas, then whipped their horses hard for several miles northeast.

Finally they figured they were far enough away from the bodies not to be connected to them should someone happen along and find them. They stopped. While Matt unsaddled and tended to the horses, Kyle built a small fire of buffalo chips and boiled some salted beef and a pot of coffee.

After eating, they took a short nap. Both they and their mounts needed the rest. Then they saddled up and rode on, arriving at the house on the Big Horizon Ranch just before dark.

Buck was about frantic. "Where'n hell you two been?" he asked, angry at himself for having worried about his brothers. He was also frustrated at having been cooped up in the house all day.

Matt bit back a retort. He had some idea of what his younger brother was going through. He explained it swiftly.

"I'm sorry," Buck said after it was told. "I should've known you weren't off lazin' around somewhere."

"It's all right, Buck." He grinned. "But me and big brother here are a mite hungry after all this idlin'."

"Clarissa says supper'll be served directly," Maybelle reported.

The maid appeared at the door to the parlor moments later. "Mistah Weymouth is at the do'," she said. She looked frightened.

"You boys stay hid," Buck said to his brothers. He stood, a look of expectancy on his face. "I'll handle this one."

He strode out, with Eula Mae hurrying after him. When he got to the front door, Buck had his Colt in his right hand. With his left hand he yanked open the door. The move shocked Weymouth.

The barrel of a Colt pistol under his nose startled him even more.

"Miss Eula has asked me to tell you not to come 'round here no more, Mr. Weymouth," Buck said tightly, but with real joy in his voice. "You ain't taken hints before, so I thought I'd be a bit more direct this time."

Weymouth gulped but said nothing. He was too afraid. That made him angry, but he would channel that anger into something else, some other time. Now was not the time to let his rage rule him.

"You understand me, Weymouth?" Buck asked harshly.

"Yes," Weymouth squeaked. He found a little courage inside. "But I'd like to hear her say it." There was a note of disdain in the words.

"Miss Eula?" Buck said over his shoulder.

"I don't want to see you no more, Colin," she said. There was no doubt in her voice or words. "I don't even want you coming 'round the Big Horizon no more."

"That clear enough for you, Weymouth?" Buck asked. He sounded contemptuous.

"Yes," Weymouth hissed.

"Good." Buck lowered the pistol, uncocking it as he did. As he dropped it in his holster, Weymouth suddenly threw a fist at him.

Eula Mae screeched in surprise and fear for her man.

"Damn," Buck muttered, as the punch knocked him back a few steps. Anger flickered in his eyes as he brought his hand to his mouth. It came away with a touch of blood on it.

Weymouth stood in the doorway, smirking. It was a mistake.

Buck charged, shoulder lowered. His shoulder rammed into Weymouth's midsection, and drove him back, across the porch. They fell down the stairs, Weymouth's back bouncing on the steps.

When they landed in the dirt, Weymouth was already moaning. Buck scrambled up. With a left hand, he grabbed a fistful of Weymouth's vest and shirt. With his right, he hurled punches at Weymouth's face and head.

Ranch hands ran out of the bunkhouse, some carrying lanterns. They stood around, not sure what to do. It was a hell of a good fight, as far as they were concerned, but still . . .

"Stop!" Eula Mae finally screamed. "Buck, stop!"

The rain of punches slowed but continued.

"Buck!" Eula Mae said more reasonably. "Let him be now. You'll kill him if you don't."

"It's my aim," Buck said quietly. But he stopped throwing fists, though he still held Weymouth's shirt and vest in his hand.

"You kill him and Sheriff Burleson'll have to arrest you, Buck. They'll hang you certain."

Buck nodded and let go of Weymouth's clothing. The Englishman fell back, his head hitting the ground. He groaned.

"Some of you boys get him on his horse," Buck ordered the ranch hands. While three men did so, Buck came up to Weymouth's horse. He looked up at the Englishman. "Don't you ever set foot on the Big Horizon again, you dumb son of a bitch. You do, and you'll leave in a coffin."

He was not sure Weymouth even heard him. The Englishman was in pretty bad shape, Buck could see in the light of a lantern. "Maybe a couple of you boys best ride along with him," Buck said. "See that he don't fall off his horse." Buck picked up his pistol, which had popped out of his holster during the fight. He holstered it, spun and headed up the stairs.

Eula Mae took his arm and walked inside with him.

"Took you long enough," Matt said as Buck and Eula Mae walked back into the parlor.

Some of Buck's anger vanished. He managed a weak grin. "Weymouth wanted to dance a little."

"Was he any good?" Matt asked.

"Nope." He sat, sighing wearily.

"You do him much damage, Buck?" Kyle asked. He didn't exactly sound worried, but there was an odd edge to his voice.

"Not too much, I reckon. Thumped him good for a while, but Eula Mae stopped me before I did him too much harm. I think. Why?"

"This might set him off, Buck. Might force him into usin' violence."

"He don't worry me," Buck said cockily.

"He should. Man like that can hire all the guns he needs. Might take him a while, but he'll get 'em."

"We can take them, too," Buck said. He no longer sounded so arrogant.

"Most likely," Matt said with a slight grin. "But you know better'n to set the odds so high when it ain't necessary. And, you got Miss Eula to think about now. And Maybelle."

Buck gulped, feeling badly now.

"Besides, we can't stay awake all the day and night. He hires enough guns—which we've been told he's been tryin' to do anyway—we'll have to be alert every minute."

Buck nodded. In his excitement, he had not thought of all the troubles he had brought. Still, he was not about to stand there and let Weymouth attack him. "I had to do somethin'," he explained. Even to him it sounded lame.

"How's your jaw?" Eula Mae asked, trying to break the tension. She touched a finger to his lip.

"Fine," he said angrily. Then he loosened up. "I'm all right."

Maybelle handed him a brimming glass of bourbon. He nodded thanks, and downed a quarter of it in one gulp. As it burned down his throat, he relaxed a little more.

He set the glass on the table and looked at his right hand. It was slightly swollen and blood seeped from a split knuckle. He shook the hand. It would heal eventually. He had done worse to his hands in brawls.

"Well," he said, starting to smile at his brothers, "since you two know so awful much about everything, what's our next move?"

Before either could answer, Maybelle stood up. "I don't know about the rest of y'all, but I'm hungry. While you were out there foolin' 'round, Buck, Clarissa was seein' to supper. I aim to eat some of it." She left the room in a swirl of skirt.

Matt laughed and stood. "I think Maybelle's got the right idea." He walked out of the room, followed by Kyle and then Buck with Eula Mae.

McFarrin, looking worried, joined them at the table. They kept their talk away from business during the meal, preferring to enjoy the food.

After supper, they retired to the parlor. Eula Mae passed drinks around to the men—and her grandmother. She also handed her father and the two older Ramsey brothers cigars. She took a cup of coffee for herself and sat.

When everyone was settled, Buck said, "Well?"

"I think I need to go see a few people in Dodge City," Matt said. His eyes glittered. "And I reckon you and Kyle ought to stay here and hold down the fort."

Buck nodded. He knew better than to argue when he saw that look in Matt's eyes. He also had enough sense to know that what Matt had said make sense. Kyle might draw too much attention, what with only one arm and his LeMat. And he had Eula Mae to worry about. Matt was the right choice here.

After a few moments silence to let the others digest what they had just heard, Matt said, "I'll leave at first light."

The others nodded.

"Who you got to see?" Buck asked.

CHAPTER

★ 20 ★

The ride to Dodge City, Kansas, was long, boring, hot, and tiring, but Matt had made good time. He had covered the roughly two hundred miles from the house on the Big Horizon Ranch in little more than three days.

Ramsey wasted little time on the dusty trail. He stopped only when he needed to so the horse could rest a bit and they both could eat and drink.

He had spent upwards of eighteen hours a day in the saddle. Because of it, he was in ill humor when he finally rode into the raucous Dodge City from the northwest. But knowing he was finally here helped perk him up some.

So did a short session in the Bear Tooth Saloon and a slightly longer session in Madame Beulah's brothel. Both establishments were in the Hell District, just south of the railroad tracks of the town.

He rode back over the tracks and into the main part of town. At the first restaurant he found he filled his belly with good, hot food, the first he had had since he had left the ranch. While traveling, he had contented himself with jerky and dry biscuits most of the time. For supper—he usually stopped well after dark—he might stew up a bit of salted beef and make a pot of coffee. But it was meager fare for such a big man, and he was glad to fill himself on the not-bad food offered by the restaurant in Dodge.

After eating, he puffed on a cigar as he rode slowly up the street to the livery. He turned the black mustang over, paying extra to see that the mount got the best care.

Then he walked up the street, looking at signs, searching for one in particular. He smiled grimly when he spotted the sign:

Headquarters
Midland Central Railroad
Lemuel Meredith, Pres.

Ramsey tossed his cigar butt in the dirt and headed up the three stairs and through the door.

The outer office was unprepossessing. A large, flat-topped desk dominated the center of the room. Just in front of it, running the width of the room, was a three-foot-high railing, the gate of which was just to Ramsey's left of the desk. Behind the rail were some cabinets for storing papers. Maps and photographs of trains adorned the walls. Several chairs were lined up against a long table against the side wall behind the desk. A potbellied stove stood in the opposite corner. A thick door stood in the center of the back wall. It was ajar, giving a glimpse at a rich office behind.

Ramsey stopped at the railing in front of the desk. While he waited, he looked over the man sitting there. The man was young and had a strict, bookish look about him. His shirt was crisply white and the sleeves were held up by black garters. He wore a green eyeshade. His hair was slicked back with grease. One delicate hand held a pen, with which he scratched in the book over which he was studiously bent. He ignored Ramsey, as if he didn't even know the man was there.

The only other man in the room was sitting in a chair tilted back against the rear wall, next to the door. He glared balefully at Ramsey. He wore wool trousers, a white cotton shirt, a plain wool vest, a tall hat, a neckerchief, and knee-length boots. He was a sallow-faced man of medium height. He was the sort of wiry man who could be very dangerous if taken lightly. Ramsey didn't take him lightly.

The man at the desk was still paying Ramsey no attention. It did little to alleviate Ramsey's renewed and growing annoyance. Ramsey coughed politely.

The man looked up, startled eyes large and round behind small, gold-rimmed glasses. "Yes?" he asked, somewhat perturbed at the disturbance.

"I'd like to see Mr. Meredith," Ramsey said politely.

"On what business?" the young man sniffed.

"I'll discuss that with Mr. Meredith."

"I'm afraid Mr. Meredith is a very busy man. He has no time for the likes of you," the young man sniffed indignantly.

"I am hot and tired and in one hell of an ill humor, boy," Ramsey said harshly, trying to control his anger.

"That's not my account," the man blinked. "We do not hire track layers or any other laborers here. You'll have to see the foreman. He's out on the line. Now, good day to you, sir." He bent his head back to his book, dismissing Ramsey.

As the young man went to dip his pen into the inkwell, Ramsey slapped a big paw over the bottle. When the railroad employee looked up at him, surprised and angry, Ramsey said tightly, "I ain't here for a job, boy. I have come a long way to see Mr. Meredith. I ain't aimin' to leave till I do."

The other man had tipped forward on his chair; now he stood up and swaggered toward Ramsey. The pearl handles of his twin Colts gleamed in the light streaming through the window over the table.

"I'll have to ask you to leave, mister," he said as he reached the railing.

"Not till I've seen Meredith," Ramsey said harshly, glaring at the gunman.

"Like Horace already told you," the guard explained patiently, "Mr. Meredith is busy." He shrugged. "But so as not to be inhospitable, Horace'll be happy to affix a time when you can come back and see Mr. Meredith."

"Of course," Horace Atwater said, relieved. "Now, let's see." He picked up another book from his desk, opened it, and glanced at one of the pages. He looked back up at Ramsey. "Yes, we can let you have a few minutes with Mr. Meredith two weeks from the day after tomorrow." He smiled blandly. His pen was poised, ready to write down the name in his book. "And who shall I say will be calling on Mr. Meredith?" He asked, the politeness oozing off him like honey from a hive.

Ramsey straightened. Atwater was no danger to him, and he wanted to keep his eyes on the guard. "You deaf? Or just stupid?" he asked, directing his words toward the guard. "I ain't goin' nowhere till I've seen Meredith."

The man stiffened. "You best leave, boy. Now!"

"Not till I see Meredith."

The man's eyes narrowed. He reached down to his side and began hauling one of his fancy Colt pistols out.

Ramsey backhanded him with his left fist, sending the gunman sprawling. The man's Colt, most of the way out of the holster, hit the floor and went skittering away across the wood.

When the guard stopped, his hand instinctively went for his other pistol.

"Don't," Ramsey warned. His own, well-used—but well-cared for—old Colt Army was in his big fist, cocked and pointed at the guard's midsection.

The man froze, but Ramsey could see in his eyes that he wanted more than anything to try it.

A well-dressed man of medium height and considerable weight stepped out of the back room. He took in the scene in one sweeping glance. "Listen to him, Temp," he said politely. When he was sure the guard would do as he was told, the newcomer looked at Ramsey. "Can I be of service, Mr. . . . ?"

"Ramsey. Matt Ramsey. You Meredith?"

The plump head nodded once, sending off a puff of Lilac Vegetal aftershave. "I'm Lemuel Meredith."

"Then I reckon you can be of service. I've rid a long ways to have some words with you. These two oafs didn't think I was fit company for you, though. We was just discussin' the merits of that opinion."

"Apparently you have made your point, Mr. Ramsey," Meredith said. He seemed to be mildly amused. "But why would you ride a long way to see me? Are you looking for work?"

"No, sir." He paused. "I have some information you might be interested in. And I have a request to make."

Meredith raised his eyebrows at him in question. "Well?" he asked after a moment.

"I expect what I got to say might be better discussed in private."

Meredith thought about that for a moment. "Where'd you come from?" he asked suddenly.

"Over near Dirt Creek, in Colorado Territory." He watched Meredith closely.

Meredith nodded, eyes narrowed in thought. *This could be trouble,* he thought. "Come in, then."

"What about him?" Ramsey asked. The pistol had not wavered from the guard's midsection. Now it waggled just a fraction to make sure there was no mistake about whom Ramsey was talking.

"My guard," Meredith said. "Jason Temple." He looked at the guard. "Temp?" he asked.

Temple scowled, but he said calmly, "You tell me to leave him be, Mr. Meredith, I'll leave him be. Unless he causes trouble in your office."

"That good enough, Mr. Ramsey?" Meredith asked.

"His word good?"

"Yes," Meredith said. There was no doubt in his voice.

Ramsey nodded. Without hesitation, he uncocked the revolver and dropped it into his holster. "I see no real need for it, Mr. Temple," he said evenly, "but should your pride be powerful hurt by what's happened here just now, I'll be willin' to give you another chance at me—after my business here is done."

Temple stood, looking at Ramsey. This was a man of honor, he thought. Temple considered himself one, too. They were much alike, he decided. And such men should not seek to kill each other without good purpose. Wounded pride was not a good enough reason. He knew Ramsey could have easily killed him a few moments ago, but hadn't. That made Temple trust the big, dark gunman.

"My pride's been hurt before," Temple said firmly. "I see no need to try and salvage it through blood."

Ramsey nodded, accepting it. He, too, was certain he could trust the railroad gunman. It was a gut feeling, instinctive. But such things had always worked for him before, he saw no reason not to trust in his feelings now.

Meredith knelt and picked up Temple's Colt and handed it to him, butt first. He made no comment as he did it. As Temple sheepishly took the weapon and slid it into his holster, Meredith turned and walked toward the rear office. Ramsey followed.

The rear office was commodious, warm, and brightly lighted from several windows. The room had good carpets on the floor and good paintings on the wall. The desk behind which Meredith sat was made of expensive wood and was highly polished. On it, at one corner, sat a lantern of fancy, colorful cut glass. The room's several chairs were plush with upholstery. Everything in the room, in fact, attested to wealth and position.

Such places once made Ramsey uncomfortable, as if he didn't belong in them. But he had spent enough time in such places, and he had enough self-esteem, that it no longer bothered him.

"Have a seat, Mr. Ramsey," Meredith said, waving a hand at a chair in front of the desk.

Ramsey took it, a little anxious about doing that, since it would leave his back to the door. While he trusted Temple, a kernel of doubt remained.

"Cigar?" Meredith asked. He rose and leaned across the desk, holding out an open boxful.

Ramsey nodded. He half rose, reached into the box, and pulled out a cigar. He drew it slowly under his nose as he inhaled deeply. It was strongly aromatic, not the foul-smelling sticks of tobacco that usually passed for cigars out this way. He nipped off the end and spit it into the bronze cuspidor on the floor by the corner of the desk. He lit it and drew in a mouthful of smoke. He puffed a few moments. "Nice," he said.

Meredith nodded.

CHAPTER

⋆ 21 ⋆

"Now, suppose you tell me what information you have about Dirt Creek that you think interests me," Meredith said. He was skeptical that Ramsey had anything of importance to tell him, but he had to hear it to make absolutely sure.

"You got a deal with a bum named Colin Weymouth?" Ramsey asked bluntly. He had no reason to beat around the bush.

"I can't say one way or the other," Meredith allowed cautiously. "Such a thing—if it existed—would be privileged information, you understand."

Ramsey nodded. "Well, I have it on good authority that it does exist. Let's say it's true then." It was a question.

Meredith nodded. He folded his hands across his portly stomach. The cigar between his teeth waggled occasionally and sent up a steady stream of billowing clouds of smoke.

Ramsey explained in detail what he knew about Weymouth's plans for the new town on the Big Horizon Ranch, his lies to the people of Dirt Creek, his attempts to get at the ranch through Eula Mae. It took some time.

When Ramsey finished, Meredith sat for a while, thinking. Still without saying anything, he rose and walked to a cupboard along the side wall to Ramsey's left. He got two glasses and filled them with good rye whiskey. He handed one to Ramsey and then sat down again. New cigars were produced and lighted.

Only then did Meredith say, "If all this is true, Mr. Ramsey—and I'm not saying it is—why should any of it concern me? Or the Midland Central? It would be a deal between the railroad and this Mr. Weymouth. How he conducts business out there would be his own affair." There was no arrogance or smugness in the voice, Meredith was just stating the facts, as he saw them.

Ramsey thought it over a minute, then said, "It ain't right that you should try to hurt the people of Dirt Creek. Even if you ain't had a hand in it directly. Nor should you be tryin' to hurt Mr. McFarrin. Ain't a one of them folks done anything to you—or the railroad."

Meredith shrugged.

"The folks of Dirt Creek are lookin' forward to havin' the railroad. Hell, they'll go out of their way to help you out, if you just ask them."

Meredith shrugged again.

Ramsey got angry, but he managed to control it. He sipped some of the excellent whiskey and puffed the fine cigar. "Word gets out, people ain't gonna think too kindly of the railroad, Mr. Meredith," Ramsey said slowly.

"People often dislike the railroad, Mr. Ramsey. For many reasons." Meredith sighed. "I'm afraid it's human nature. There's always some folks who feel that the railroad is hurting them in some way. Taking their land, bypassing their town, whatever." He shrugged. He could not help those things. "There are many who feel that progress is to no one's advantage, certainly not theirs. They seem to think that anything that is good for the railroad is bad for them." He sighed.

Ramsey nodded. "I reckon that's so. But you're dealin' with an Englishman here. A foreigner. Many a folk won't look favorably on such a thing. Many might see that as an attempt by some foreign king to gain control of American interests. Might cause a hell of a stink was folks to get hurt."

For the first time, Meredith showed a little doubt. He had had the same thoughts when Weymouth had approached him with the possibility of a deal. He had let himself be talked out of it, figuring most of the people way out there in Colorado Territory would not be able to see that likelihood. But now he wasn't so sure.

"Does the railroad really need that kind of trouble?" Ramsey asked slyly. "Most railroads got enough troubles just from the nature of the business without goin' out and askin' for more."

Meredith was beginning to get a little angry. Partly he was angry that the situation had arisen. Partly, though, he was angry at himself for letting it develop as it had.

Seeing that Meredith was wavering, Ramsey pressed on. "And what'd happen should officials out in the territory find out about this?" he asked quietly. "There's talk that Colorado will become a state soon. The first governor, whoever he turns out to be, might not look too kindly on an Englishman runnin' a heap of land in his state."

That would certainly foul the railroad's progress, Meredith thought. What he knew, and he supposed that Ramsey didn't, was that statehood for Colorado was a done deal. Statehood would become official within weeks. Meredith wanted no part of anything that might cause him grief with the new state government.

Most railroads got a certain amount of free land wherever they were planning to build. The railroads would sell the land to raise money for construction and such. A governor who was angry that his constituents were being hurt by the railroad—in favor of some foreign royalty, no less—could very well be disastrous to the Midland Central. And that, in turn, could be disastrous to him, personally and financially.

The more he thought about it all, the angrier Meredith got. Not only was this becoming an unbearable situation, Meredith realized that he did not like being lied to. He was a deal-maker, the man who usually pulled the strings. To realize he had been manipulated by a young son of some minor British nobleman galled him to no end.

Still, he was a little wary of Ramsey. What did the gunman want out of all this? What would he get? Meredith did not want to just cancel the whole deal with Weymouth, without something to take its place. He did not want to be hurt himself nor the railroad, which was his creation.

"Accidents could happen to someone who caused such troubles," Meredith said. He had no plans on having Ramsey killed, but he wanted to see how Ramsey reacted to it.

"Accidents can befall anyone," Ramsey said pointedly. "Besides, something happened to me, there's others to take my place," he added with a shrug of his broad shoulders.

Meredith nodded in understanding. The point had been made, and now it was discarded. He hadn't wanted to do that anyway, since he was beginning to like this big, rugged Texan.

He sighed. "The Midland Central does have a deal with Mr. Weymouth," Meredith said cautiously. "I'll admit that much. Exactly what it calls for, I won't say. However, to cancel that deal might mean great financial and other hardships for the railroad. I have . . ." He paused a moment.

"I have some misgivings about just reneging on the deal," he said after a moment. "You can understand that, can't you? It would be very costly to the Midland Central to renege. There would be lawsuits and angry recriminations. Considering Mr. Weymouth's station, a foreign government could become involved." He raised his arms as if to indicate he was helpless in all this. "And with nothing with which to replace the . . . considerations . . . we have in the arrangement with Mr. Weymouth, well . . ." Again the rounded shoulders rose and fell.

Ramsey nodded. "I understand. You have to look out for yourself and the railroad and the investors. I don't. All I got to look out for is my family." He smiled a little. "My youngest brother is sweet on Mr. McFarrin's daughter, and we've been friends with the McFarrins for some time. That makes them practically family. I don't much give a damn about the folks in Dirt Creek, though I sure as hell hate to see innocent folks hurt for no reason."

Ramsey paused. He finished off his whiskey and set the glass on the edge of the desk. "I figure, though, that if you help us out here, that the people of Dirt Creek would be mighty grateful to you. It'd serve to build you up a heap of good will, not only around Dirt Creek, but . . . well, if word got out that the Midland Central cared about folks, I reckon it'd serve you well in other places."

Meredith nodded slowly, warming to the thought.

"And," Ramsey went on, "if the spot where Weymouth was figurin' to put a new town is really the best site for a station and town, well, I'm quite certain that Mr. McFarrin will be more than happy to offer up a portion of his ranch for a new town—for the right price, of course."

"Of course," Meredith murmured. He liked Matt Ramsey; he thought him honest but far-sighted enough that his honesty could not be exploited too far. Caring for people—especially ones a person didn't know—usually was a serious flaw in a man, Meredith thought. But somehow it seemed proper in Ramsey. Meredith also figured Ramsey for the type of man who would do everything in his power to hurt the Midland Central Railroad if Meredith did not cooperate. Meredith was not afraid of a political or court fight with Ramsey, or the town of Dirt Creek, or even the entire state of Colorado. He was fairly certain he could win most of those battles.

But Lemuel Meredith was a pragmatic man. He could see no benefit in court fights or unnecessary political maneuverings, nor could he see any benefit in prolonging the deal with Colin Weymouth. He was smart enough, too, to know that many people already thought poorly of all railroads. Too many railroads—including his own—had been constructed without regard to the people they would touch. It created plenty of resentment. Meredith thought it extremely wise to go against that grain right now, to develop some good feelings in the people along the route of the Midland Central. It could boost the railroad considerably.

Meredith had great plans for the Midland Central Railroad. He envisioned trunk lines crossing Kansas, Nebraska, Colorado, Wyoming Territory, maybe even to places like New Mexico Territory and Utah Territory, the mines of Arizona Territory. If he dreamed hard enough, he could see lines running all the way to the coast of California. He could picture himself as the premier railroad man in all of America. It was a pleasing thought. And the little corner of the world known as Dirt Creek, Colorado Territory, could very well be his stepping stone to such greatness.

"Horace!" he bellowed.

A moment later, Horace Atwater raced into the room, his face even more pale than usual. "Yes, sir?" he asked, worry evident in his voice.

It did not take long for Meredith to explain to his clerk and secretary what he wanted.

"Yes, sir, Mr. Meredith," Atwater stuttered. "Right away, sir." He grimaced. "It will take a little time, though." He was afraid Meredith would have him shot.

"I understand. Will first thing in the morning be enough time?"

"I would think so."

"Make sure it is." Meredith waved his hand, dismissing Atwater, who hurried out, shutting the door softly behind him.

"You have a room for the night, Mr. Ramsey?" Meredith asked.

"Hadn't thought that far ahead." He shrugged. "I imagine I can find one."

Meredith wrote for a minute, the pen's scratching loud in the room. Meredith blotted the paper, then folded it. "Go on over to the Gold Spike, up the street here two blocks, turn left, another block up. Give this to Wilburson. Your night's lodging will be free. As will everything else." He grinned pleasantly. He might be a man who thought little of others most times, but when he took to someone, he was generous. He had taken to Ramsey because Ramsey had gotten him out of a potentially very damaging predicament. Without cost. He felt it proper to be expansive in such matters.

"Everything else?" Ramsey asked, hoping it meant what he thought it did.

"Food, drink." He grinned impishly again. "Women. The Gold Spike has the finest women between St. Louis and San Francisco. They will be at your disposal for the night."

"Obliged, Mr. Meredith," Ramsey said, smiling. He stood and grew more serious. "For everything."

Meredith shrugged. He, too, stood. "I did little."

"That ain't true, and you damn well know it," Ramsey said seriously. He stuck out his hand.

As Meredith shook Ramsey's hand, he realized that Ramsey was more astute than he had given him credit for. He understood that Ramsey knew what he was thinking. It raised his respect for Ramsey considerably. It also made him even more glad that he had made this new deal with Ramsey. He would keep the deal, too, he vowed to himself. He knew that crossing Ramsey would be very foolish—and probably fatal.

Meredith nodded. "Have a good evening, Mr. Ramsey. You come back first thing in the morning. Everything should be—will be—ready."

"Obliged, Mr. Meredith."

CHAPTER
★ 22 ★

"You best get a little rest, Buck," Kyle said quietly one afternoon. He and his brother were in the barn, caring for the horses. He set down the bucket of water he was carrying and looked at Buck.

"What for?" Buck asked, surprised. He stopped pitching hay and jabbed the pitchfork into the pile. He rested his gloved hands on the top of the hilt and looked over it at his brother.

"It's been three days since you thumped Weymouth. I expect he's had time to recover enough to start drummin' up trouble, was he of a mind to."

"Night riders?" Buck asked.

"It'd be likely. We ain't been to town, and I don't think he's got the gumption to come against us in the daylight. Hell, he ain't got the gumption to come against anybody in the daylight, I'd wager. I'd expect that son of a bitch'll figure a couple night raids'll be enough to scare you off."

"Me?"

"He still don't know about me," Kyle said with a wide grin. "Nor Matt. He's still thinkin' you're out here alone, with maybe some of the ranch hands to help out."

Buck laughed. "Be a hell of a surprise for him when he comes around, won't it?"

"I hope." He paused. "Now, you go on and rest. I'll finish up the chores."

Buck nodded and headed toward the house. McFarrin had given each of the Ramseys a room upstairs. As he reached the stairs, Buck stopped only long enough to kiss Eula Mae briefly. She looked at him in wonder as he headed up the stairs.

Halfway up, he decided she needed some kind of explanation,

but he didn't want to frighten her unduly, either. He turned on the stairs and said, "I ain't used to all this hard work. It's been a time since I did such things. I figured I'd go on up and rest a spell."

Eula Mae smiled at him. She didn't believe him, and she suspected something was up. It was not like him to either be lazy nor to nap in the afternoon. But she could not force him to tell her anything.

Buck had a little trouble sleeping, but finally managed to doze off. Kyle woke him in time for supper. After the meal, McFarrin sent the women off, and the three men sat sipping whiskey in the den. McFarrin had been considerably more friendly with Buck since their talk. He seemed to have relaxed some, too, which Buck thought might account for some of his change in attitude.

"Kyle says he expects trouble soon, Buck. Do you agree with that?"

"Yes, sir."

McFarrin nodded. "I think you're right. Kyle has asked me for a few ranch hands to keep watch over the place with you boys each night. I've agreed. Bryce and Klemmer will be on with you tonight. The others will, of course, come runnin' should the situation call for it."

"Sounds right," Buck allowed. Bryce and Klemmer were steady hands. They weren't maybe the best shots in the world, but they were coolheaded enough, as far as Buck could tell. Klemmer had fought in the war—for the North, but such things were behind them all now.

"Well," Buck said, standing, "reckon I best get on outside. Bryce and Klemmer ready?"

"Should be waitin' over to the bunkhouse," McFarrin answered.

Buck nodded and left. He spent most of the night riding Biscuit around the ranch near the house, patrolling the road and the rolling prairies nearby. But he was still out of position when the attack came.

Suddenly there was a whoop and a holler and maybe a dozen riders swooped down toward the ranch house, barn, and bunkhouse. Gunshots rang out in the starlit night. Several men stopped to light already made torches.

The torches were thrown at the buildings while gunfire continued to ring out. Then the invaders scattered, riding hard into the night.

Cowboys poured out of the bunkhouse. Buck and Klemmer galloped up almost at the same time, as the McFarrins ran out of their house. Bryce rode up minutes later. Fire was licking at all the buildings but had not taken firm hold yet.

McFarrin shouted orders, and the men formed bucket brigades at each of the three buildings. Pails of water were scooped up from big wood horse troughs and passed hand to hand until they were splashed on the bright flames.

Within minutes, the fires were out. The cowhands and McFarrin headed back to their beds. As Buck pulled himself wearily onto Biscuit, Kyle walked up to the horse and looked up at his brother. "You'll be all right, Buck?" he asked.

Buck nodded. He rubbed a hand across his face. "Damnit, Kyle, it was like they knew when we wouldn't be right here. I feel like a goddamn fool."

"I know how you feel, boy. But it can't be helped." He paused. "If it'll ease you any, I don't figure they'll be back tonight. This had the look and feel of a raid meant to frighten rather than to kill."

"Folks could've died in those fires."

"Hell," Kyle spat. "I saw 'em as I was comin' down the stairs. They were all firing their guns in the air. I reckon it was to make sure we were all awake, so we could fight the fires. Except for the barn, the fires were set in places that would take a little while to really get started. I think they just wanted to scare the livin' daylights out of Artemis, Maybelle, and Eula."

"What about me?"

Kyle grinned. "I expect they figured that a scared Eula Mae would convince you to leave."

"Shit," Buck muttered. But he smiled as he pulled Biscuit's head around and trotted off.

The next night was more of the same. But Kyle, who was more attuned to such types of things, seemed to sense when the riders were coming, and he fired off two or three shots to warn everyone else just after the riders passed his position twenty yards from the house.

Because of it, fighting the flames was somewhat easier. In the light of the next morning it was found that the two nights of raids had done little actual damage. Still, it did not make living on the Big Horizon any easier.

Things took a turn for the worse when Tolbert Hill, McFarrin's ramrod, rode up in the early afternoon. His horse was lathered, and the ranch hand came off the horse before it hardly had time to stop. Everyone inside heard the noise and came out to stand on the porch.

"What's wrong, Tol?" McFarrin asked. He had never seen his foreman in such a state. Hill was usually calm and even-tempered.

Hill pulled off his battered Stetson and wiped his forearm across his sweating forehead. "I don't figure it's fit for women's ear, Mr. McFarrin," he said quietly.

McFarrin nodded. "Eula, you and Mother Sweet go inside," he ordered.

"But, Father."

"Don't sass me, girl," McFarrin snapped. "Do it!"

When the two women had gone into the house, McFarrin said, "All right, Tol. Spill it."

"Found four head dead this mornin', Mr. McFarrin." He winced. "Includin' Minotaur."

Buck looked at Hill blankly.

"Minotaur's one of our prize bulls."

"Damn. How?" McFarrin asked. He thought it odd, though some strange things could happen. Maybe they were all snake bit or had caught some disease. Such things had been known to occur, though it was unlikely.

"They was shot," Hill said flatly.

"Jesus Christ," McFarrin snarled. He stood there silently, almost shaking with rage. He could barely think, he was so angry. It was one thing for Weymouth to send his men against the house to try to frighten them, especially since McFarrin, the Ramseys, and the ranch hands were prepared for it. But to shoot a man's herd down, to attack his very livelihood, was more than the simple ranchman could believe.

McFarrin managed to bring himself under control after a few minutes. He nodded. When he spoke, it was in calm, measured tones. "All right, Tol. Get all the hands and get your asses out on the range. Round up every head of cattle you can find. Bring 'em to Horse Valley. Leave a couple of hands there to watch over 'em. Tell the boys to kill anyone who comes around tryin' to bother the herd."

"Yes, sir. Anything else?"

McFarrin rubbed his jaw as he thought. Then he nodded and said, "Yeah. Start to the east and southeast. That's nearest Dirt Creek, where we can expect men to come from. But don't spend too long at it. I want you and everyone else back by nightfall. I don't think the raiders are gonna take the night off. Just get as many head you can as far out as you can and still get back here by dark."

"Yes, sir," Hill repeated. He started for his horse.

"Wait," McFarrin commanded.

Hill looked back and McFarrin said, "Best cut yourself a new horse. That one's spent."

Hill nodded and pulled himself on the horse and rode toward the corral behind the barn. He was a true cowboy, had been on a horse since he was a toddler. He never willingly walked anywhere.

"Damn," McFarrin muttered again. He looked at the Ramseys. Buck looked fresh, but Kyle had been awakened by the noise after having patrolled all night. He was disheveled and ragged looking.

"I think this has gone far enough," McFarrin said tightly.

Buck nodded. "Yep," he said quietly, firmly. Eula Mae was a nervous wreck, though she was trying to hide it. And when such things started getting to his woman, he got angry.

"We ride over to Weymouth's, then?" McFarrin asked.

Buck started to agree, but Kyle said sharply, "No." When the other two looked at him, he said, "We go over there and do some damage, they'll hang all of us sure as shit. We've got no proof he's mixed up in all these doin's. Even though we know it to be true. Besides, I'm hopin' Matt'll be able to get us the proof we need to end it."

"Then what should we do?" Buck asked. He was edgy. He wanted action, but at the same time, he wished this was all over and he could get on with his life. "Nothin'?"

"No," Kyle said, a slow, vicious grin crawling across his lower face. "We set us a little trap for Mr. Weymouth's night riders."

Kyle headed up to his room and lay on his bed for a while, thinking. The kernel of a plan began to jell, and he finally drifted off to sleep. When Buck woke him for supper, he knew what had to be done. It was not a great plan, not a deep plan. But he figured it was workable.

After supper, Kyle outlined it to Buck and McFarrin. Then he added, "I reckon we ought to keep it quiet from the hands, though."

"You think some of 'em's mixed up in this?" McFarrin asked. The thought was inconceivable to him.

Kyle shrugged. "Wouldn't be the first time some poor-assed cowpoke has had his head turned by a pouch of money, Artemis."

McFarrin nodded. "So it's just the three of us, then?"

"Yep. Buck'll go out and ride, just like the other night. Soon's Bryce and Klemmer are off ridin' somewhere, he and I can take our positions up."

"And me?"

"You stay in the house here to protect the ladies, should that become necessary."

McFarrin nodded again. "You think it'll work?" he asked, suddenly feeling uncertain about it all.

Kyle shrugged. "I'm hopin' that if we do a little damage to them, they'll be discouraged from comin' back." He dropped his cigarette into the nearby cuspidor. "And, if that don't discourage 'em, at least we'll have evened up the odds a wee bit."

CHAPTER

★ 23 ★

Buck pulled himself onto Biscuit, trying to temper the flames of excitement that flickered in his heart. He settled his behind into the saddle.

"Bryce," he ordered, "you head west, then arc around to the north and then back. Klemmer, you go the other way and do the same."

The two hands nodded solemnly and moved off slowly, weaving rhythmically in their saddles with the ease of men who had been born to horseback.

Buck moved off slowly, too, onto the road leading to Dirt Creek. He rode down it as far as the sign that announced the Big Horizon Ranch. He waited there for more than an hour, yawning occasionally as he fought off the desire to sleep. He saw nothing out of the ordinary. He turned eastward, moving slowly over the swells in the land.

The land glimmered oddly under the bright half-moon and the thick carpet of stars. He curled around, across a meandering line of mud that was occasionally a stream, and headed in the general direction of the ranch house. But before he got there, he dipped into a slight gully and then came up behind the corral and barn.

He stopped and tied Biscuit to the top rail of the corral, keeping the barn between the horse and both the house and the bunkhouse. Then he moved along the back wall of the barn, to the side nearest the road. He peered around the corner. Spotting no one, he crept along that wall and then checked again at that corner. Still no one was seen.

Quickly Buck went back and got Biscuit. He walked, towing the horse, retracing his steps. Around the northern side, he slipped into the dark barn through the wide double doors.

Buck tied Biscuit to a post and patted the faithful horse's neck. Then he slid the Winchester out of the scabbard. Climbing the ladder with the rifle in hand was no easy trick, but he finally stood in the hayloft. He moved swiftly to the east side and eased open the hay doors. It gave him a good view of the house, the eastern sweep of plains, and a fair section ambling off to the southeast.

He stood, rifle in his right hand, his left bracing him on the edge of the hay door. He saw the front door of the house open a little. He couldn't see inside, of course, but he waved the rifle.

A moment later, Kyle came out of the house, from the back. He ran, crouched, through the garden and then down into the stream bed. It was mostly mud and sand now, with little pools of water. He moved down it, following the bed southward to a point beyond the barn. He rested near a bush in a dip a few yards off the road.

The night lagged, with neither Ramsey moving much. But an hour or so after Kyle came out of the house, Buck spotted a rider over to the east. He was moving fast. "Klemmer," Buck muttered. But he wondered why the ranch hand was galloping hell-bent for leather.

Buck stared at the dim figure, trying to discern some features of the man so far away in the dim light. But he could not. He blinked a few times, trying to get his eyes working again after the long staring into the night. When he stopped that, the rider was gone, having disappeared behind a knoll.

Buck heard a rumbling, like a herd of horses or cattle running. He stared out down the road. In a few moments, he spotted riders. They pulled up suddenly, the dust visible as an eerie silver cloud in the moonlight. A single rider came from the east—the man Buck had seen earlier. The man stopped with the group.

What they did, then, Buck did not know. As suddenly as they had all stopped, the riders started again, heading at a dead run for the house.

"They're comin', Kyle," he said, not loudly. He didn't want to alert anyone but Kyle. He just hoped that Kyle had heard him.

"I'm aware," Kyle said quietly, his voice drifting faintly up from down by the stream.

"They're on the road," Buck said again, still keeping his watch.

As they neared the ranch house area, some of the riders started veering off, spreading out from the road. Some stayed on the road; none slowed his pace.

"They're fannin' out, Kyle," Buck called urgently. "Off the road."

"Which side?" Kyle sounded calm.

"Both."

"Cross-fire," Kyle said.

Buck knew it was the only way. He checked the Winchester over again, though it was unnecessary. He leaned against the left edge of the hay doors and leaned partway out. He brought the rifle up. The riders were within a hundred and fifty yards of him. In the daylight, it would be an easy shot, and he would not hesitate a moment. But at night—even one fairly brightly lit like this one— he would not chance it.

So he waited. He kept his aim on one man, following him down the road, waiting, waiting. . . .

The riders got to within less than a hundred yards. Buck still had the man in his rifle sights. "Damn," he suddenly muttered. "Bryce, that son of a bitch."

He fired, and Bryce toppled back off his horse. Buck quickly levered another round into the chamber and fired again.

All hell seemed to break loose. Buck fired as rapidly as he could, but with too little effect after the first couple of shots. The darkness, the fast-moving riders, the cloud of powder smoke in front of his face, the return fire that erupted all conspired against him.

In the midst of the cacophony, Buck could hear the heavy cough of Kyle's LeMat letting fly a burst of buckshot occasionally, and the higher pop of the nine-shot revolver. At one point, out of the corner of his eye, Buck saw Klemmer charge up on his horse.

Suddenly the night riders were fleeing, racing either down the road or across the plains. Riderless horses milled about near the barn; others raced off after the mounted animals.

Buck waited briefly, to make sure all the riders who could were fleeing. Then he hurried across the loft and half slid, half climbed down the ladder. He ran outside.

McFarrin was on the porch, a pistol in one hand, lantern in the other. Most of the ranch hands were edging down toward the barn. They, too, were armed.

"Kyle?" Buck called loudly.

"Here and all right," the one-armed brother shouted back. "You best come on over here and see this."

Buck headed around the barn toward his brother. McFarrin hurried to catch him. Eula Mae and Maybelle stood in the doorway, looking out. The ranch hands moved up en masse.

Kyle was kneeling over a body.

"Bryce!" McFarrin exploded. He looked at Buck in anger. "Did you know about this, Klemmer?"

"No, sir," Klemmer stammered, uneasy in the glare of his boss's eyes.

"You, Buck?"

Buck shook his head. "Not till I blasted him off his horse just now." He sighed. He supposed either he or Kyle should have suspected something. But Bryce had never given any indication; he had always appeared to be what everyone thought he was—a hard-working, butt-poor ranch hand.

Kyle said, "Let's go take a look at the others."

They found another man dead, and three wounded, none of those seriously. They dragged the bodies into the barn and marched the wounded men in after them. The wounded were tied, standing, to poles in the barn.

"You know any of them, Mr. McFarrin?" Kyle asked.

"Nope. Except Bryce, of course." He paused, running a hand through his thinning gray hair. "Well, what're we gonna do with this bunch." He waved his thick hand at the wounded men.

"Shoot 'em," one of the ranch hands mumbled.

There was a grumble of agreement from the other hands. They were hard men, used to a rough and unsettled life. They did not take kindly to men riding onto their ranch—as they might see it—to raise hell, scare the daylights out of the womenfolk, burn down the living quarters, and in other ways endanger them. It wasn't right, and these men were not the type to let such things pass without seeking some kind of retribution.

"It's a thought," McFarrin allowed. He had been a rancher for a long time, and a cowpuncher before that. He had lived on the Texas frontier for most of his life and was as hard as any of his men. But he had not gotten to be where he was by letting his heart rule his head. "But I reckon not, boys," he added. "We'll let 'em cool their heels here for the night and send 'em into the doc in Dirt Creek in the mornin'."

McFarrin looked at the three wounded men. They were not ranch hands. They looked more like hired guns. Not the best hired guns, maybe, but hired guns nonetheless.

"I expect," McFarrin said with a short, vicious grin, "that we could ask 'em some questions, though, while we await the dawn."

Most of the ranch hands settled for that.

McFarrin turned to leave. "Just don't go too hard in your questionin', boys," he said as he headed out of the barn.

"Why don't you go take a ride around the place, Buck," Kyle said. "See if there's any stragglers."

"What're you gonna do?" Buck looked at his brother skeptically.

"See what these three sons of bitches have to say," Kyle said flatly.

Buck nodded. He got Biscuit and walked outside. Mounting, he rode on, glad to be out in the open. He had no real desire to stand and watch a bunch of angry ranch hands trying to pound information out of three wounded men.

The excitement for that night was over, however. As dawn crept over the land, Buck headed wearily toward the house. When he got there, the ranch hands were just finishing loading the three wounded and trussed-up raiders into the back of a farm wagon. The two bodies were already loaded. As Buck climbed down out of the saddle, two cowhands climbed onto the wagon seat. One drove; the other kept his shotgun loosely trained on the captives.

"Learn anything, Kyle?" Buck asked.

"Not much," Kyle allowed. He was tired and hungry. "Those boys did 'fess up, though, that they was hired by Weymouth. And, like we figured, they were just comin' to try'n scare hell out of everybody here."

"Well, I expect he'll leave us be now that we've buried two of his boys."

"So I had thought, too, Buck," Kyle said. He was tired and annoyed. He was not much of a one for watching the wounded men get beat up by the ranch hands, but he figured he needed to be there to hear what the men had to say, if anything. He wiped the sleeve of his good arm across his sweaty face. "Now I ain't so sure, though," he added.

"Why?" Buck asked, startled. They had discussed this, and thought they had it all figured out.

Kyle shrugged. "Ain't sure. Those three didn't say nothin' directly, but I got the feelin' that once Weymouth hears he's lost two men—and maybe those three, too, if they decide they've had enough—he's gonna be madder'n blazes."

"Think he'll come lookin' for trouble?"

"I doubt he will, the yellow bastard," Kyle said in contempt. "But I suspect he'll be sendin' as many men as he can round up.

And," Kyle added with a grimace, "they won't be comin' to scare folks this time."

Buck looked grim. "Then, by God, we'll give 'em another surprise. One they won't forget."

Kyle grinned viciously. "I expect so." He scratched his nose. "It sure as hell ain't gonna be pretty, though. I wish there was some way we could head 'em off before they got here. It's too dangerous for the womenfolk."

Buck had not thought of that before, and now he was suddenly worried. "Maybe we can send Eula and Miz Maybelle somewhere."

"Where? Can't send 'em to Dirt Creek. Hell, they'd be worse off there than here. And there ain't no place else nearby we could take 'em."

"Denver?"

"Christ, Buck, that's a couple hundred miles—as the crow flies. Most of the Cheyennes've been pacified from what I hear, but that don't mean there ain't some of 'em still roamin' around causin' mischief."

"Don't I know it," Buck said fervently.

When Kyle looked at him in surprise, Buck hastily explained about his two encounters with Iron Shield and the other Cheyennes.

Kyle nodded. He chuckled a little, saying, "Hell, you got an affinity for attractin' Indians, don't you, boy? Fought Comanches, got mixed up with that Cherokee girl and her greatgrandpa, those dealin's we had with Jules . . ."

"Hell, Jules don't count," Buck grinned. "He was only a half-breed."

"Well, his wife wasn't." Kyle grinned back. "And now these dealin's with Cheyennes. Lord, boy, you'll be an Indian expert before long."

"Shoot," Buck said. He was still laughing, but there was some truth to Kyle's statements. "You ain't done so bad in attractin' Indians yourself, big brother." He was a little afraid to mention it, considering how Kyle had felt about Cherokee Lil, but he hoped his brother was over her by now.

Kyle smiled. There was joy in the smile at the remembrance of Cherokee Lil, and sadness, too. The memories were bittersweet. "Hell, she was only a half-breed, too," he said, smile growing a little.

Buck nodded. "Well, if we're expectin' trouble, we both best get as much rest durin' the day as we can."

"Yep." Kyle wiped his sleeve across his face again. "You need help with the horse?"

"Nope. Won't be but a few minutes." He looked over at McFarrin, who was talking to several ranch hands. Buck shrugged and walked Biscuit into the barn. He quickly unsaddled the horse, curried him, and then made sure there was plenty of grain and water in the mount's stall.

When he came out of the barn, Kyle fell into step beside him as he headed for the front porch.

CHAPTER

⋆ 24 ⋆

It was a long boring night, and one that brought no action for the residents of the Big Horizon Ranch. As dawn eased its way over the landscape, Buck rode up from the southeast, and Kyle from the northeast. They met near the barn's gaping doorway.

McFarrin strode out of the house and marched to where the Ramseys had just dismounted. He was grinning from ear to ear. "Looks like we showed that damned Weymouth," he crowed. "Scared his ass right off here once and for all." His puffy, white muttonchops fairly quivered in victory.

"Don't be so sure of that, Artemis," Kyle said. He grimaced.

"Hell," McFarrin snorted. "Weymouth's got no spunk. He's been scared off good. Don't you worry about him no more." McFarrin strode off, beaming, filled with purpose and good feelings.

"You ain't thinkin' the same way, are you, Buck?" Kyle asked as the two men led their horses into the barn.

"Nope." Buck had anticipated action and was feeling almost let down that none had occurred. He knew, though, that Weymouth would send his men against the ranch again. It made some sense to wait a while. For one thing, that would be likely to make the ranch residents react just as McFarrin had—with overconfidence. For another thing, Weymouth might need time to recruit more men or to just replace those that had been lost.

"Good." Kyle strained and grunted in unsaddling his horse. Like most other things, it was not easy with only one arm. He persevered, though, as he had since it had happened so many years ago in the war.

When the horses were unsaddled, curried, fed, and watered, the

Ramseys headed out into the blazing heat of the yard, making their way toward the house.

"Damn, I'm hungry," Kyle said with a grin.

"I am, too." Buck relaxed, letting the tensions flow out of him. He felt even better when Eula Mae met him at the door and escorted him to the breakfast table.

After a filling breakfast of slab bacon, eggs from the chickens housed in coops behind the house, biscuits and jam, and coffee, the two Ramseys headed for their rooms. At the top of the stairs, they stopped.

"When do you think Matt'll be back, Kyle?" Buck asked.

Kyle shrugged. "Ought to be any time, I reckon. Unless he's run into trouble somewhere. 'Course it's hard to tell just how long it was gonna take him to get to Dodge in the first place. It's a pretty fair haul, I'd think."

McFarrin thought the Ramseys were crazy when they set their drinks down after supper and headed for the door. "Come on, boys," he said jovially. "There ain't gonna be no more trouble." He had not felt this good since he had come to Colorado.

"That might be true," Kyle said. "And I sure as hell hope it is." He paused. "But I ain't . . . I'll feel a heap more comfortable was me and Buck to spend another night or two out there. Just in case."

McFarrin knew there would be no arguing with either Ramsey. "You two want some help?" he asked. "I can have a couple of the boys help out."

The Ramseys looked at each other. Kyle shook his head, and Buck said, "Reckon not, Mr. McFarrin. They'll be around should something happen. No reason they should lose any more sleep than they have already."

McFarrin nodded. "I still think y'all're fools, though." He grinned and held up his glass of bourbon, half saluting them, half enticing them to rejoin him in the relaxation.

The Ramseys nodded and left. They were silent as they walked across the yard to the barn and saddled their horses. They rode out of the barn and stopped. It was another warm, clear, moon-lit night.

The brothers did not have to say anything. Buck simply went one way and Kyle the other.

Buck was off to the north a few hundred yards beyond the house when he heard the rumble of horses again. He had heard it that once, the night before last. He didn't think he would ever forget it. He remembered when he was still a boy, just after the war. Kyle and Matt had come back, far different from the men they had been when they left. Buck listened to them talk occasionally with other veterans of that conflict. More than once they had described the sound of the rush of horses coming at them, how it was a distinctive sound and one that did not fade easily from the memory.

Buck slapped his reins on the ginger-colored horse and charged for the house. He wondered where Kyle was.

He raced through the garden, heedless of any damage he caused. He thought he saw lanterns flicking on in the house, but he wasn't sure. Several gunshots rang out.

He yanked the horse hard and skidded around the corner of the house. He slowed but did not stop. But within a moment he had assessed the situation. Riders were pouring toward the yard from the west, firing as they rode. He spotted Kyle charging in from the southeast, splattering across the muddy stream.

The next thing he knew, he was falling out of the saddle, a sharp pain spreading out from the left side of his chest. He hit the ground hard and grunted from the impact and dropped the Winchester he had been carrying. "Jesus," he muttered. "Damn!"

Biscuit trotted off, leaving Buck lying there.

As soon as he was able, he reached up and felt his chest. His relief at not finding his hand wet with blood was as great as his astonishment at that.

He heard Eula Mae scream, "Buck!"

Only seconds had passed since he had been shot off his horse. He leapt up and spun toward the house. Eula Mae had run out the door and across the porch with Maybelle right behind her. As she reached the stairs, Maybelle grabbed her granddaughter. Bullets tore up splinters of wood from the porch, posts, and steps.

Suddenly Eula Mae screamed again as Maybelle fell, knocked backward by some force. The girl leaned over her grandmother, screaming.

As Buck ran toward the two women, he scooped up his rifle and glanced at the battlefield, taking it in in one sweeping look.

Cowhands were boiling out of the bunkhouse, guns out. Most of them had been in gun battles like this before. They quickly melted into the shadows and began sniping at the night riders.

Kyle was kneeling halfway between the bunkhouse and the ranch house, firing his LeMat steadily.

Buck reached the women. Eula Mae was crying crazily, oblivious to almost anything that went on around her. Worried about her, Buck found that he couldn't be too concerned about the bullets still flying around. He glanced at Maybelle. The top half of her dress was wet with blood. She was awake and alive, but Buck could not tell how long she might stay that way.

"Get her into the house, Eula!" Buck shouted over the din.

Eula Mae paid him no heed.

"Damn," Buck muttered. He yelled for McFarrin, who was kneeling on the porch, firing over the railing. When McFarrin looked at him, he shouted, "Get Maybelle into the house. Now!"

McFarrin came running. As the ranchman lifted the old woman in his arms, Maybelle moaned. Buck was sure she'd be dead within minutes.

"Sons of bitches!" Buck bellowed. He whirled and snapped the Winchester up to his shoulder. He fired the rifle as fast as he could jerk the lever up and down.

Night riders were falling fast. Buck could tell that, though it was difficult to see anything anymore. Between a few high clouds that had moved in, the thick veil of dust from horses' hooves, and the pall of powder smoke, one could hardly see anything.

The Winchester ran out of ammunition, and Buck threw it on the porch. He yanked out the Colt, crouching and waiting for a target.

They were few and far between now, though. What riders were left were fleeing fast. As the wind began to clear the air, Buck could see them racing off, after having heard them.

Then it was silent. Or so it seemed after the cacophony of the battle. Kyle strolled up to his brother. He went through the one-armed ritual of ejecting the spent shells from the LeMat and reloading it.

"You all right, little brother?" Kyle asked while he worked. It was something of a joke between them. Buck was as big as Kyle now. He might be eight or so years younger, but he was not quite Kyle's little brother any longer.

"I expect so." Now that the battle was over, his rush of adrenaline was slowing. With it came the awareness of pain in his chest. He pulled open his shirt and the top of his longjohns and looked inside. In the dim light of the moon and the house lanterns, he could see a bruise spreading.

"Hurt?" Kyle asked. He looked concerned but not real worried.

"Took a bullet in the chest," Buck said with a tight grin.

Kyle looked at him, eyes raised questioningly.

In the heat of the battle, Buck had not thought of it since it had happened. Now his hand accidentally touched his pocket. He smiled amidst it all when he felt his combination folding knife. It had a knife, fork, and spoon that folded up into the handle. He usually carried it in his saddlebags, but he had used it earlier in the evening to eat a can of peaches as he rode. Afterward, he had absently dropped it in his pocket.

He reached into his pocket and pulled out the utensil. It was broken in half. "Wasn't for this, I expect I'd be layin' out there with those others." He waved a hand at the bodies littering the yard. He reached in his pocket again. A moment later he pulled out a flattened, spent bullet. He shook his head in amazement. Then he dropped the bullet and broken knife back into his pocket.

"Shit," he suddenly muttered.

"What's wrong?" Kyle asked. He was worried now.

"Maybelle!" He spun and ran across the porch. Kyle was only a few steps behind him. Grabbing his rifle on the run, Buck burst into the house and ran down the hallway and into the parlor. Eula Mae and McFarrin had placed Maybelle on the long sofa.

"How is she?" Buck asked, breathlessly. He was worried about Maybelle. He liked the old woman, had from the first they met, and would hate to see her go under now, like this. Now that he was over the blinding rage he had felt outside, he could worry about her.

"I'm fine, damnit," Maybelle muttered. She slapped McFarrin's hand out of the way when he tried to keep her down. "I'd be right sprightly if these two vultures weren't hoverin' over me just awaitin' my untimely end."

Buck laughed in relief. "I'll be damned," he whispered.

"I expect you will," Maybelle said, an edge of contrariness in her voice.

"But I saw you covered with blood out there."

"Hell, it was just a scratch. We'll fetch the doctor out here tomorrow, if such is needed. For now, I'll have Clarissa poultice it up." She pushed McFarrin out of the way. "Now where's my corncob?"

Everyone looked around at each other, shrugging with bafflement. Finally Eula Mae said, "I'll check outside."

"We best see to some things outside, too, Buck," Kyle said quietly.

Buck nodded. This would not be pleasant, cleaning up after a battle like this never was. "You stay here, Eula," he said. "I'll check on Granny's pipe."

"But . . ."

His look stopped her. He didn't want her to see what was out there, and she had just realized it. She really didn't want to see it, either.

While Buck poked around on the porch, looking for the pipe, Kyle headed out into the yard.

The cowhands were standing around, talking, smoking their rolled cigarettes, joking softly, awaiting orders. "Let's start draggin' those bodies over here, boys, and see what we got," he said, almost cheerily. After some of the battles he had been in—including Vicksburg where he had lost his arm—this would be nothing.

"Where you want 'em?" Tol Hill asked.

"Lined up against the road side of the barn'll do, I expect. That'll let us still have a little light to check 'em, but it'll keep 'em out of sight of the house."

The hands nodded. They could understand that the women should not be subjected to such things.

"We gonna have to bury 'em all?" someone asked. The question was followed by a burst of low laughter.

Kyle thought a moment, then shrugged. "Don't see why y'all should. Once we get 'em sorted out, we'll toss 'em in a wagon and haul 'em into Dirt Creek. Let the undertaker worry about it."

"Hey, what if we find any live ones?" someone else asked. There were no chuckles this time.

Kyle shrugged again. "I'll leave that to you boys," he said quietly. "To your consciences."

The ranch hands dropped their cigarettes in the dirt and headed in different directions.

Buck had found Maybelle's old corncob pipe and brought it inside to her. He came back outside just as the hands were moving off. In the short time he had been gone, he had worked up another head of steam. Seeing Maybelle's pale face and blood-covered clothing enraged him. He could not believe the raiders had shot at the women.

"I think we got to end this, Kyle," he said bitterly. "Soon."

"Yep." Kyle watched the men dragging bodies toward the barn. He glanced casually when he heard a gunshot, and he shrugged. "Bastards probably deserved it," he said barely audibly.

He sighed. "We'll cart this riffraff into Dirt Creek tomorrow. Then we'll pay Mr. Weymouth a visit, I think."

Buck's eyes glittered in the moonlight. He nodded acceptance.

CHAPTER

⋆ 25 ⋆

The bodies were piled into a large farm wagon. There were seven of them, all told, and they were thrown on the wagon like so much dead wood.

Three wounded men climbed into the back of the wagon, behind the bodies. They looked bewildered. They were not really hardened gunmen. They might have liked to be, but that was before the massacre last night. Now they were simply glad to be alive, and they hoped to stay that way. The three bloody, bedraggled young men just wanted to get away from here and try to get on with their lives—without requiring a gun. They had had quite enough of that.

Two cowboys tied the wounded men to each other and then to iron rings bolted into the sides of the wagon.

The two Ramsey brothers stood on the porch of the house with McFarrin, watching the goings-on. The ranch was showing some semblance of normality, with most of the hands heading out to the pastures. The blacksmith was busy at work in the barn. Pigs wallowed and chickens cackled out behind the house. A dusty summer breeze did little to alleviate the budding heat.

Tol Hill rode up to the porch and dismounted, his lanky frame loose. "Them varmints is ready for haulin' off to Dirt Creek, Mr. McFarrin," he said laconically.

McFarrin nodded. Hill mounted and walked his horse away, spurs jingling softly, chaps flapping in the breeze.

"Well, boys, I expect it's time we paint the tiger," McFarrin announced.

"We?" Kyle said, looking at him with one eyebrow raised. "You ain't goin' anywhere, Artemis."

"But I expected . . ."

"I know what you expected. But this is your home. You'll stay here and defend it—should that become necessary."

McFarrin grumbled, then said, "It ain't right that you do this. This here's my fight more than it is yours." He looked adamant.

"It's our fight now," Buck said flatly.

"Colin Weymouth was my enemy long before he was yours, Buck," McFarrin snapped. "Or yours, Kyle." He was no longer much of a fighting man, but there had been some times when he was younger. . . . And he still liked a little excitement now and again.

"Don't matter," Kyle said quietly. "This has gone far beyond some minor feud, Artemis." He shook his head. "This is war now, plain and simple. You ain't equipped for it. Me and Buck are."

McFarrin looked from one Ramsey to the other. Their big, broad faces, so similar in color and texture, were flat and determined. McFarrin knew in his heart he was overmatched in the fight with Weymouth, but he hated to seem weak in front of men such as these, or in front of his family. What's more, he saw in the Ramseys things he did not possess: qualities of recklessness, of fearlessness. They were, plain and simple, warriors. He was not.

McFarrin nodded. "Then at least take some of the hands with you."

"Just two—to drive the wagon."

"You might need help," McFarrin warned.

"We'll handle it," Buck said. There was a note of cockiness in his voice.

Hill rode up again. Without dismounting, he said, "Rider's comin'."

The Ramseys turned sharply.

Kyle's hand went up to help his hat shade his eyes. "It's Matt," he said, voice evidencing a touch of excitement.

Matt rode slowly past the wagon, looking at it with a mixture of curiosity and dismay. The dismay was because he evidently had missed some action. He touched his hat as he passed the ranch hands standing around. Most of them quietly returned the greeting.

Matt stopped near the foot of the porch stairs. He stretched his back wearily, and rolled his neck. "Looks like you had yourselves a pretty good fandango here while I was gone."

"Reckon it broke the monotony some," Kyle offered.

"Anyone killed?"

"None that counted."

"Hurt?"

"Miz Maybelle got winged. It ain't slowed her none." Kyle grinned. "None at all. Same with Buck."

Matt returned the smile. "What's with the wagon?"

"Just gettin' ready to make a little delivery to Dirt Creek," Buck said, smiling viciously.

"And then?" Matt knew his brother was not finished.

"And then," Buck said with a tight grin, "we were fixin' to go callin' on Mr. Colin Weymouth."

Matt nodded. "I don't expect you boys'd like some company, would you?"

"Oh, I don't know," Buck said with a chuckle. "What do you say, Kyle? Think we got any need for some old, broke down saddle tramp with a bad humor and a slow gun hand?"

Kyle rubbed his face, pretending to mull it over. He was getting into the spirit of it. "Well," he finally said, "I don't rightly know." He squinted up at Matt. "He looks kind of moth-eaten." He seemed to get downright cheery. "But, what the hell, I reckon if he's that bad off, he'll be an easy target. Maybe those hardcases'll concentrate on him and leave us to do the real work."

"Might," Buck said thoughtfully. "Well, if you want him to drag along, I reckon I got nothin' bad to say about it."

Matt was laughing. He dismounted. "Well, shoot, since I'm so old and decrepit, I reckon you boys'll have to wait a spell before we leave. Old codger like me will need some grub, maybe a nap."

McFarrin stood watching Matt walk up the three porch steps. He shook his head in wonder. The Ramseys were about to ride off and face God knows what; two of them had been in a hell of a battle the night before, in which seven men had died; they had been ready to drag a wagonload of bodies down into town. Yet here they were joking like this was a church outing. He didn't understand it. He thought it interesting, but he didn't understand it.

"Best make it a short nap," Kyle said with a laugh. "Them bodies out there are gonna be gettin' ripe soon considerin' the heat and the sun."

"Maybe I can skip it, just this once." Grinning, he shook hands with both his brothers and then McFarrin.

"Good to have you back, big brother," Buck said seriously. Though he and Kyle were the closest in looks, it was with

Matt that he shared the most inside. They were of the same temperament. Buck always felt comfortable with Matt around.

"Glad to be back." He pulled off his hat and slapped it against his leg several times, raising up little clouds of dust. He squinted at Buck. "Somethin' ailin' you, boy?" he asked sharply.

Buck grinned shyly. "Almost bought the farm last night." He explained about the bullet.

Matt grunted. "You're one lucky son of a bitch, ain't you." He would not let his relief show.

"Well?" Buck asked impatiently after several moments of silence.

"Well what?" Matt asked blandly. He had put his hat back on but was still slapping dust off his clothes.

"Damnit, Matt," Buck said, a note of friendly warning in his voice.

Matt grinned. He walked back down the steps and reached into his saddlebags. He pulled out a sheaf of papers bound by cord. He waved them around before putting them back. "Got everything we need to end Weymouth's schemin'," he said as he marched back onto the porch.

Buck's right hand tapped the Winchester he held in his left. "I got everything I need to put an end to his schemin' right here."

"Might come to that," Matt admitted. "From the little I've seen about the way Weymouth acts, it most likely will. But with those papers, it can be done legally. We'll turn 'em over to the judge in Dirt Creek. Then we'll see what happens with Weymouth. He comes for us, we can take him down with a clear conscience—and keep our asses out of the calaboose at the same time."

"Reckon you're right," Buck grumbled. He hated it when his brother was so obviously right and he was so obviously wrong.

Kyle nodded. "Best get movin'. Those dead fellers over in the wagon ain't gettin' any fresher."

"Whoa, there, brother," Matt said. "I been up ridin' all the night just to get here. I ain't so old that I need a nap 'cause of it. But I am hungry." He looked at McFarrin. "Think Clarissa could rustle me up somethin', Artemis?"

"Of course." He turned and walked purposefully into the house.

"You two mind waitin'?" he asked, addressing his question to his brothers.

Both shook their heads. "Hell, we hardly ate anything ourselves," Buck said. "I could do with another flapjack or two."

Matt nodded and turned. He called Tolbert Hill over. When the foreman arrived at the bottom of the stairs, Matt said, "Please have someone see to the black. He's been ridden hard and needs care. I'll need him again soon's I'm done eatin'."

Hill nodded.

"One more thing, Tol. Those saddlebags contain some very important papers. I'd be more than a little put out was somethin' to happen to 'em."

Hill did not look impressed. "They'll be safe," he said. He leaned over and took the black's reins. He rode slowly toward the barn, calling for a couple of hands.

The Ramseys walked into the house. Kyle and Buck went to the living room, while Matt plodded upstairs to his room. The tiredness was catching up to him, but he knew that once he had eaten, and the excitement of pending action crept up on him, he would be fine. Inside his room, he tossed his hat aside.

He wished he had time for a bath—he was covered with sweat and dust. But he didn't. He splashed water into the bowl from the pitcher and washed his hands, face, and neck. That improved his spirits some right off. He unbuttoned the filthy cotton shirt and took his only extra one out of a dresser drawer. He pulled it on and tucked it in. With a new bandanna around his neck, he headed for the dining room.

The meal was a mostly silent one. Matt chowed down. He had not been lying about being hungry. He had not had a real meal since some time the day before. He was too busy eating now to talk much.

Buck and Kyle were about talked out, at least on the subject of Weymouth. McFarrin was content to sit, sip coffee, and puff on a fat cigar.

Maybelle and Eula Mae were subdued. Eula Mae knew the trouble was not over, and she was worried about what might happen. The Ramseys might joke in the face of danger, but the woman knew that any moment one of them could die. Eula Mae thought she would die, too, if something happened to Buck.

Maybelle was feeling a little sore from the wound. It was a shallow rip along her ribs and would not incapacitate her much. But right now it hurt like hellfire, and that made her cranky. So, she, too, kept mostly silent, lest she vent some of her crankiness on men she admired and who might be facing death any moment.

Finally Matt was finished eating. He shoved back in his chair, patting his stomach in contentment.

"You have time for a cigar before you boys leave, Matt?" McFarrin asked. "And perhaps another cup of coffee?"

Matt looked at his brothers. Kyle nodded acceptance. Buck was impatient to be on the way, but he forced himself to relax. He nodded tightly.

Matt lit the cigar McFarrin gave him and nodded thanks when Clarissa refilled his cup. The maid filled everyone else's, too. They sat quietly.

Seeing that Matt's cigar was about smoked down, McFarrin raised his coffee cup. "God ride with you, boys," he said solemnly.

The Ramseys polished off their coffee, accepting the salute. Then Buck stood. He might be the youngest, but he had earned his rights among the Ramseys. "Let's ride," he said. Then he headed out the door.

His brothers were right behind him. Their horses were saddled and waiting by the porch, tied loosely to the hitching post. Kyle and Buck pulled themselves into the saddles. Matt checked his saddlebags for the papers. Satisfied, he climbed onto the black.

They moved out at a fast walk, the wagon rattling and bouncing along behind them. The three wounded men looked faintly sick, after having been sitting in the back of the wagon while the bodies bloated under the hot sun for more than an hour.

On the road they settled into a steady, even pace. Each Ramsey rode immersed in his own thoughts, seeing the possibilities in his own way.

CHAPTER

★ 26 ★

The Ramseys sparked a considerable amount of attention among the townsfolk of Dirt Creek. The three walked their horses slowly up the shabby main street of the town, followed by the plodding wagon. The Ramseys appeared to be ignoring the people who stopped and stared at the procession. But in reality, they had never been more alert. Their eyes swept from side to side, anticipating danger from all angles.

They all stopped near the doctor's small, pitiful office. One of the cowboys on the wagon cut the three wounded night riders loose. He jerked his head in the direction of the physician's, a few doors down a side street that might more properly be called an alley.

The procession lurched on again, stopping soon after when Sheriff Woody Burleson suddenly appeared in the middle of the street. He cradled a shotgun in his crossed arms.

Burleson pointed at Buck. "That man is an escaped prisoner, with a multitude of crimes to answer for. Not the least of them being wholesale murder." A short, skinny finger pointed at the wagonload of bodies. "Best come with me now, Buck, before there's more trouble."

"You don't get out of the way, Sheriff," Matt said calmly, "you'll be joinin' those in the back of the wagon."

"And at least two of you punks'll go with me." Burleson was astounded that Buck had come back to Dirt Creek.

Matt's Colt leapt into his hand, and a bullet kicked up a puff of dirt inches from Burleson's right foot. Burleson tried to cover up his surprise with only some success.

"As I was sayin', Sheriff, y'all best move yourself, 'less you're fixin' to find a place in the Eternal."

"What's your interest in all this, Mr. Graham?" He smiled weakly. "I've heard about the visit you and your brother there made to The Ranchman."

"Name's not Graham, Sheriff," Matt said coldly. "Just used that name to get in there and check things out some. My name's Ramsey. Matt Ramsey. This is my brother, though," he added, indicating Kyle. "As is Buck."

Burleson nodded. It all made a lot more sense now. "What do you want here?" He was nervous but hoped it did not show.

"Where's Judge Waverly?" Matt asked.

"His office," Burleson answered. He was startled again, wondering what the Ramseys would want with the judge. "Why?"

Matt ignored the question. "Where's his office?"

Burleson half turned and pointed.

Matt nodded, and moved his horse forward slowly, shoving past Burleson, who snarled as he jerked out of the way. The other two horsemen rode by him, too. Burleson considered using the shotgun in his hands but then decided this was not the time or place. He watched as the wagon clattered past, then he spun and walked after the parade.

At the town hall—a long grubby place of sod and adobe—the Ramseys stopped. Matt dismounted first. He walked up to the wagon that had stopped just behind the Ramsey's horses. "Take this refuse over to the undertaker's," he ordered. "If he gives you any guff, unhitch the team and take 'em home. Leave the wagon—and the cargo—out back."

Both ranch hands nodded slowly, unconcerned. The wagon pulled away, the driver clicking at the horses and slapping the reins as he made a wide turn.

Matt stopped alongside his horse. In a moment, he had extracted the bundle of papers from the saddlebags. He stepped up onto the boardwalk in front of the town hall.

"Get out of the way," Matt growled at Burleson, who had planted himself in front of the door.

"No," Burleson said, nervously. "I've got to know what's goin' on here." He started bringing the shotgun out of the crook of his arm. He froze when he felt the muzzle of Buck's Colt brushing his temple.

"I'll take that," Kyle said gruffly. He grabbed the shotgun.

"You want to know what this is all about, come on," Matt

said. He looked at his brothers. "You'll make sure we ain't disturbed."

The two nodded and took up positions on each side of the door. Matt opened the door and waved for Burleson to precede him. Burleson shrugged and walked inside, with Matt right behind him.

The two were gone less than half an hour. With the exception of one outburst that the two Ramsey outside could faintly hear, it had been quiet, both inside and out. Buck and Kyle glared at anyone from the town foolish enough to stare at them for more than a few seconds. That was enough to send them uncomfortably off.

They were also alert, waiting for something to happen. They had made plenty of enemies in town, and with Weymouth living just over the hill, they figured that sooner or later the Englishman would send some men over to find out what the Ramseys were doing in Dirt Creek.

Finally, Burleson and then Matt stepped out of the doorway. Matt no longer had the sheaf of papers. Burleson looked bewildered, as if someone had just performed a magic trick right in front of his eyes and he could not believe it happened.

"It took some talkin', but you're off the hook, Buck," Matt said. There was no joy in his voice; he had expected nothing less.

Buck nodded, not showing the relief he felt. "What now?" he asked.

"Now we go lookin' for Mr. Colin Weymouth and his compadres," Matt said tightly. He looked at Burleson. "Sheriff," he said, "I'd suggest you get folks off the streets. I expect trouble'll be commencin' before long, and I'd hate to see any innocent folk get hurt."

Burleson nodded. "You need help?"

"None but what I just told you."

Burleson was considerably relieved. He was not a cowardly man, but he wanted no part in the bloody war that was coming to a boil. He had no stake in either side winning—or losing. Not as long as he kept a middle course. He had tried to do that all along. He admitted he had to stagger off that line every so often. But he always wandered back to it.

He stepped down off the sidewalk and started yelling at the nearest people, telling them to get off the street and under cover. The people began to move off and Burleson followed, spreading his word of warning throughout the town.

The Ramseys waited until the streets were empty of all but

themselves. The breeze blew steadily, stirring up the dust along the street. It also brought the smell of manure and garbage with it.

"Let's go," Kyle said. As the oldest, and having been the one who had commanded men in the war, it was Kyle's right to give the orders now.

"Where we gonna find Weymouth—and his men?" Buck asked.

Kyle shrugged. "Shouldn't be hard."

It wasn't. They stepped off the steps, leaving their horses there and headed in the direction of The Ranchman. But before they had got a dozen yards, an armed Colin Weymouth came strutting up the street with seven gun-heavy men arrayed behind him. The two groups stopped facing each other, fifteen or twenty yards between them.

"You three chaps—whoever you all are—have caused me quite enough trouble here," Weymouth said.

"We," Buck said proudly, "are the Ramseys." He paused an instant. "And y'all will become well-acquainted with us soon, Weymouth, if you don't get your ass out of Dirt Creek now, and never come back."

Weymouth laughed, trying to seem lighthearted. But the sound was brittle. It cracked and splintered in the hot summer air. "You will see what real power is, you foolish young buffoon." He grew angry. "You will feel my might." He raised a clenched fist in front of him. "I will crush you with it."

"Your days here are over, Weymouth," Kyle said coldly but calmly.

Again came the fractured laughter. "Surely even you can see the foolishness of such a statement."

"We—and all the folks 'round these places hereabouts—have had our fill of you and your schemin', Weymouth," Buck said.

"Then you fellows may leave," Weymouth said with what he thought was calm reasonableness.

"It's you who'll do the leavin', Weymouth," Matt said. "And hell, we'll even give you a choice. You can leave on your own two feet. Or in a pine box."

The men behind Weymouth began to shift, spreading out a little for some operating room. In response, Buck, on Matt's left, levered a round into the Winchester, Kyle, on Matt's right, lowered the sheriff's shotgun and braced the butt against the front of his hip.

Things were quiet, though the wind blew in puffs, bringing to them the clapping of a loose board, the rattle of harness chains, a burst of raucous laughter from a saloon.

Then one of the men behind Weymouth shrugged. "This ain't my fight no more, boys," he said tightly. He spun and walked toward the building to his left.

Another one nodded. "Reckon he's right." He headed for the saloon on the opposite side of the street. With a start, Buck recognized the voice as that of the third man who had tried to kill him in the dark outside the Red Dog Saloon a few weeks ago.

Two more men—one to each side—began to follow the first two.

"Stop! All of you!" Kyle snapped. His voice was commanding.

The four men did as they were told. Each turned to face the Ramseys. One grinned viciously. He had wanted to get to the trough over by the building, so he had some protection. But if he couldn't, at least he and the other three had spaced themselves out considerably—almost all the way across the street. It would make it very difficult for the Ramseys to concentrate on them that way. Not with the other three men—and Weymouth—in the middle.

"What is it going to be, gentlemen?" Weymouth asked. He smirked, standing with his thumbs hooked into the watch pockets of his fancy vest.

"That's up to you, Weymouth," Matt said. "Tell your boys to put down their pieces, then you come along peaceable over to the jail house, and nobody'll get hurt."

"Should I choose not to do such a foolish thing?"

Matt shrugged. "Then there'll be blood spilled."

"You are considerably outnumbered, chaps. It would seem I have the upper hand. So, perhaps *you* fellows would like to lay down your weapons?"

"What in hell would we do such a goddamn fool thing for?" Buck asked, surprised. He was utterly sure he and his brothers were in the right and had no doubts that they would prevail. He could not conceive of giving up.

"Why, to save your miserable souls," Weymouth said. He laughed for the first time in some minutes. It was stronger than the last time.

"I expect savin' our souls ain't very high on your list of things to do, Weymouth," Kyle said. "Now, let's cut the crap. Y'all either give up now or . . ." He let it hang in the breeze.

"I see," Weymouth said. He paused, as if thinking.

The Ramseys were not lulled.

"I'm afraid, gentlemen, that I have other plans, and surrender ing is not my way . . ." He nodded once sharply before gliding backward a few steps so he was behind some of his henchmen.

Weymouth's seven gunmen went for their pistols. The two nearest the sides of the street dived for cover.

Kyle fired the shotgun from the hip, one barrel right after the other. He tossed the weapon away and jerked out his LeMat. At the same time, he spun and raced for the corner of the Red Dog Saloon. He stood in the alley, stump resting against the wall of the saloon. He edged the LeMat around the edge of the building and fired.

Buck was snapping shots off from the Winchester, laying down a covering fire. He hoped it would keep the seven—eight, if one counted Weymouth, which he didn't—gunmen from aiming or firing calmly. With desperation shots, they might not be too accurate.

Matt stood rooted in the center of the three, patiently firing his Colt. But five shells didn't last long in a battle such as this. As his pistol emptied, he reached for the extra he had tucked into his gunbelt at the small of his back.

"Go, Matt!" Buck roared. "Head for cover!"

Matt spun and raced toward a barrel sitting out front of the general store to the right. He set the extra revolver atop the barrel. As he scrunched down, jamming new shells into his Colt, he yelled, "Come on, Buck!"

The Winchester was out of ammunition, so Buck needed no more encouragement. He ran for some crates near the barrel in front of the mercantile store. He was breathing hard as he started pulling shells from his cartridge belt and stuffing them into the rifle's magazine.

Silence fell for a few moments. The Ramseys surveyed the battlefield as they reloaded. Four men lay dead in the street. Two gunmen were crouched behind a water trough on the same side of the street as Kyle, another was lying in a farm wagon across the street from those two. Weymouth was behind the wagon.

"You got one last chance, Weymouth," Matt shouted.

His only answer was a shot by one of the gunmen behind the trough. The sniping picked up again. Glass in nearby windows shattered, and chunks of sod or adobe flew off buildings.

At one point, as he half rose to fire a couple of shots, Buck saw Weymouth running around the corner of a building. A few moments later, Weymouth raced across the street and headed hell-bent away from town almost due west across the countryside.

"Damn," Buck snapped, crouching back down again.

"What's wrong?" Matt asked distractedly. He thought perhaps his brother was wounded, but if he was it didn't sound serious.

"Weymouth's takin' off."

"Where?" Matt asked. He had been reloading his Colt again and not paying attention to the street for that brief time.

Buck told him.

"Well, hell," Matt snapped. "Go after him, Buck. Me'n Kyle'll take care of these others."

Buck nodded.

CHAPTER
★ 27 ★

Buck ran hard back down the street, heading for his horse. All the while he ran, he awaited a bullet in the back. But Matt and Kyle kept up a steady enough fire to keep the enemy gunmen behind their cover long enough for him to reach his horse.

He stuffed the Winchester into the scabbard and jumped on Biscuit. He scooted across the street and around the curve opposite the town hall. Within moments he was past the buildings and racing across the prairie. He caught a glimpse of Weymouth a mile or so ahead. Buck slapped the reins on the ginger's sides, urging the powerful mount to full speed. The rhythmical drumming of the horse's hooves was almost soothing to Buck despite the adrenaline coursing through his veins.

It didn't take long for the powerful Biscuit to close the gap with Weymouth's delicate mare. In fifteen minutes he was within a hundred yards of the fleeing Englishman. Ramsey stopped on a long, bumpy knoll and pulled his Winchester. The horse was breathing heavily but seemed eager to run again.

Ramsey brought the rifle up, aiming to take the Englishman down with a long shot and be done with it once and for all. But something stayed his hand. He wasn't sure what it was. It was not that Weymouth was fleeing and Ramsey would have to shoot him in the back; Ramsey had done that before. And if anyone deserved killing, it was Colin Weymouth.

Ramsey finally decided he wanted to get Weymouth alive, if possible. It would be better for justice's sake. It would be, Ramsey realized instinctively, far worse for Weymouth to be brought in, thrown in jail, and convicted. The shame would be devastating.

He shoved the rifle away and slapped the horse. Biscuit responded immediately with a burst of speed. "Only a little more, boy," he whispered to the animal.

In minutes he was edging up to Weymouth's rapidly tiring horse. He pulled alongside the Englishman's left. He reached out with his right hand and grabbed Weymouth by the collar of his jacket. He yanked.

Weymouth yelped and tumbled backward off his horse as Buck let go. Weymouth landed, bouncing in the dirt and grass, grunting and cursing.

As soon as he had dumped Weymouth, Ramsey reached out and took hold of the mare's reins. He slowed, easing the other horse back, too, until they swung around in a small circle and headed back. Ramsey dallied the riderless horse's reins around his saddlehorn as he reached Weymouth. He slid out of the saddle.

Weymouth burst up from the ground, coming up low and hard. He grabbed Ramsey around the knees and dumped him. Ramsey grunted with surprise. He thought Weymouth would have had all the fight knocked out of him by now. He also was a little surprised at Weymouth's strength.

Weymouth had squiggled half on top of Ramsey, and his hands scrabbled frantically for Ramsey's throat.

"Damn you," Ramsey bellowed. He jammed a thumb into one of Weymouth's eyes and then slammed a hard forearm into Weymouth's throat.

Weymouth groaned and slumped sideways. Ramsey shoved him all the way off. Ramsey stood, rage burning through him. Much of it was anger at himself. Weymouth deserved no second chance. Ramsey knew now he should have killed him straight off. The Englishman had been responsible for numerous deaths, had almost killed Maybelle, and had scared hell out of Eula Mae. He kicked Weymouth viciously in the side and stepped back a pace.

Weymouth sucked in a breath at the sharp pain and he grimaced. Then he made a move for the pistol at his hip.

"I'd be real obliged was you to do that, Weymouth," Ramsey hissed in anger. "Then I'd not have to shoot you dead in cold blood." His hand rested on the Colt at his own hip.

Weymouth breathed out and dropped his hand. He fell back, breathing hard, as pain flooded his body.

Ramsey pulled his Colt. Aiming it at Weymouth's head, he edged up to the Englishman and knelt at his side. He pulled

Weymouth's revolver and tossed it off into the grass. He rose and stepped back. "Get up," he ordered.

Weymouth stood up. He was unsteady, but upright.

"Turn and walk toward your horse."

"What if I don't."

Ramsey sighed. "I should've shot you a couple of times. I won't hesitate again."

Weymouth smirked. "You won't shoot me," he said. There was a note of arrogance in his voice. He was of royal blood. This uncouth American would never dare to shoot him. So he thought, until he looked into Buck Ramsey's cold blue eyes. He turned and walked slowly toward his horse.

"Stop," Ramsey ordered when Weymouth was alongside his horse. Ramsey moved up and pulled the Englishman's saddlebags free. He tossed them aside. He did the same with Weymouth's fancy English sporting rifle. He mounted Biscuit and undallied the reins of Weymouth's horse.

"Mount up. Then move on out slowly. I run you down once, I can easily do it again."

"You're taking me back to Dirt Creek?" Weymouth asked, surprised.

"I aim to."

Weymouth laughed. It was a sickly sound that quickly deteriorated into coughing. "You fool," he said when the short spate was over. "The law in Dirt Creek will do nothing to me." He laughed again, cautiously, as if he were afraid of starting to cough again.

"The people of Dirt Creek know all about you now, Weymouth," Ramsey said in a voice raspy with anger. "The railroad sent all the papers along that detailed what you had planned. Judge Waverly has 'em. You'll get nothin' but trouble in Dirt Creek now, you son of a bitch."

Weymouth looked at Ramsey, his face twisted by impotent rage.

Ramsey grinned insolently back. "Move," he said, feeling some joy for the first time in a while.

They plodded along, neither speaking. Suddenly Weymouth whirled in his saddle, a small pistol in his hand. He fired.

"Jesus," Ramsey muttered as a bullet sliced across his ribs on the side. He instinctively jerked when it happened, and he could feel himself sliding out of the saddle. At the same time, Weymouth fired again.

Ramsey landed with a thud and his pistol fired. Without thinking about it, he had cocked the hammer in anticipation of taking a shot at Weymouth. The impact had caused his finger to jerk. The bullet hit nothing but dirt.

As the second bullet fired by Weymouth tore into the earth near him, Ramsey thumbed back the hammer and fired. Then again.

Both slugs caught Weymouth in the chest, one high, one low. Weymouth moaned low and gutturally. His head slumped, and then he toppled off his horse.

Ramsey rose and walked cautiously to Weymouth. The Englishman was not breathing. Ramsey shook his head. So much death, he thought, and much of it because he had wanted to do the right thing and bring Weymouth to justice rather than to just shoot him down.

He knelt and picked up the pistol Weymouth had used. It was a .32-caliber, three-shot Marston pocket pistol. Ramsey flipped open Weymouth's coat and saw the small holster sewn into the lining.

"Damn," Ramsey spat in irritation. He should have checked Weymouth over. He should have shot Weymouth. He should have done a lot of things. He snorted in disgust. Then he laughed, tired of denigrating himself. Everything had worked out for the best.

Ramsey rose, uncocked his Colt, reloaded it, and put it away. He peeled open his shirt and looked at the wound. It was just a small trail of blood. It stung a little but didn't really hurt much. He rebuttoned his shirt. With a grimace of annoyance, he bent, lifted Weymouth's body, and tossed it unceremoniously across the Englishman's saddle. He quickly sliced off the saddle strings and used the leather thongs to tie the body haphazardly.

The adrenaline was leaving him, replaced by exhaustion. Yawning, Ramsey mounted Biscuit. Taking the reins to Weymouth's horse in hand, he trotted toward Dirt Creek. As he rode, he wondered if Matt and Kyle were all right. He had plenty of faith in their abilities, but things could always go wrong somehow. He spurred the horse a little, increasing his speed some. Suddenly he was anxious to get back to town.

He trotted into Dirt Creek, unwilling to acknowledge the kernel of worry that sat in his stomach like a week-old lump of rancid bacon. He slowed, wondering whether he should stop by the undertaker's first and drop off the body, or head for the sheriff's office and let Burleson—and, hopefully, his brothers—know what had happened.

But Kyle and Matt were waiting alongside a building on his approach to the center of town.

"Wouldn't he come along peaceable?" Matt asked.

"Nope." Buck shook his head, relief at seeing that his brothers were all right canceled by a new dose of self-loathing. "Thought he would. Damn." His irritation grew. "I should've checked him over, but I didn't. He pulled a pocket pistol and winged me. That's when I ended his troublemakin'."

"Had to be done," Kyle said.

"Should've done it earlier."

Kyle shrugged. "You was tryin' to do right."

Buck smiled wanly. "Reckon you're right. I suppose you boys had no trouble."

"Nope," Matt said. "We rubbed another one out and winged one. The last decided it would be best for him to surrender while he was still all in one piece. The wounded one quit, too. They're both over in the calaboose."

Buck nodded. "Well, I best get Weymouth over to the undertaker's. Why don't you go tell the sheriff, or the judge, about it. I'll meet you there and we can head home."

"Your wound?"

"Just a scratch."

Kyle grinned. "A mite anxious to get back to the Big Horizon and see that little gal of yours, ain't you?"

Buck smiled. "Don't mind sayin' that I am. And"—the grin widened—"just 'cause you're too damned old and ugly-faced to get yourself a pretty gal, don't mean you should make fun of those of us who're young and handsome enough to do so."

"Shoot," Kyle said with a laugh, joined by his brothers. He swatted Buck on the leg with his hat. "Just get goin'."

The next few days were hectic for everyone. Buck and Maybelle spent some time recovering from their wounds.

In addition, officials from the Midland Central Railroad showed up at the Big Horizon Ranch. After a day or two of negotiations, Artemis McFarrin sold a section of land—the one near the spring—to the railroad to build a station and a town.

The next day, McFarrin and the Ramseys rode on into Dirt Creek. After talking with the mayor and Sheriff Burleson, a meeting was called. The Ranchman was chosen, and all the men in Dirt Creek were invited. Drinks were passed around and the meeting was called to order. It was a short meeting. The mayor gave a quick rundown of what had gone on and told the people about McFarrin's sale to the railroad.

Things were mighty gloomy in the fancy saloon after that. Then McFarrin stood up. His address was quick and to the point. He explained why he had sold the land to the railroad—the water. Then he invited everyone in Dirt Creek to move to the new town as it grew and take up their businesses there.

That was greeted with a cheer and considerable relief. The mayor even suggested that the new town be named McFarrinville. McFarrin grinned and said modestly, "There's time enough for such things later."

Summer was drawing to a close, and a touch of the fall could be felt in the air. Buck Ramsey watched, uncomfortable in his new wool suit, bought just yesterday from the general store, as Artemis McFarrin escorted his daughter down the aisle of the poor, shabby church in Dirt Creek.

Eula Mae arrived at his side, and Buck beamed as he turned to face the preacher. His two brothers, also uncomfortable in their new suits, closed ranks behind him. Maybelle moved up next to her granddaughter.

"Dearly beloved," the preacher intoned, "we are gathered here . . ."

America's new star of the classic western

GILES TIPPETTE

author of *Hard Rock, Jailbreak* and *Crossfire,*
is back with his newest, most exciting novel yet

SIXKILLER

Springtime on the Half-Moon ranch has never been
so hard. On top of running the biggest spread in
Matagorda County, Justa Williams is about to become
a daddy. Which means he's got a lot more to fight for
when Sam Sixkiller comes to town. With his pack of
wild cutthroats slicing a swath of mayhem all the way
from Galveston, Sixkiller now has his ice-cold eyes
on Blessing—and word has it he intends to pick the
town clean.

Now, backed by men more skilled with branding irons
than rifles, the Williams clan must fight to defend
their dream—with their wits, their courage, and their
guns. . . .

Turn the page
for a preview of
SIXKILLER
by Giles Tippette

Available now from Jove Books!

It was late afternoon when I got on my horse and rode the half mile from the house I'd built for Nora, my wife, up to the big ranch house my father and my two younger brothers still occupied. I had good news, the kind of news that does a body good, and I had taken the short run pretty fast. The two-year-old bay colt I'd been riding lately was kind of surprised when I hit him with the spurs, but he'd been lazing around the little horse trap behind my house and was grateful for the chance to stretch his legs and impress me with his speed. So we made it over the rolling plains of our ranch, the Half-Moon, in mighty good time.

I pulled up just at the front door of the big house, dropped the reins to the ground so that the colt would stand, and then made my way up on the big wooden porch, the rowels of my spurs making a *ching-ching* sound as I walked. I opened the big front door and let myself into the hall that led back to the main parts of the house.

I was Justa Williams and I was boss of all thirty-thousand deeded acres of the place. I had been so since it had come my duty on the weakening of our father, Howard, through two unfortunate incidents. The first had been the early demise of our mother, which had taken it out of Howard. That had been when he'd sort of started preparing me to take over the load. I'd been a hard sixteen or a soft seventeen at the time. The next level had jumped up when he'd got nicked in the lungs by a stray bullet. After that I'd had the job of boss. The place was run with my two younger brothers, Ben and Norris.

It had been a hard job but having Howard around had made the job easier. Now I had some good news for him and I meant him to take it so. So when I went clumping toward his bedroom that was just off the office I went to yelling, "Howard! Howard!"

He'd been lying back on his daybed, and he got up at my approach and come out leaning on his cane. He said, "What the thunder!"

I said, "Old man, sit down."

I went over and poured us out a good three fingers of whiskey. I didn't ever bother to water his as I was supposed to do because my news was so big. He looked on with a good deal of pleasure as I poured out the drink. He wasn't even supposed to drink whiskey, but he'd put up such a fuss that the doctor had finally given in and allowed him one well-watered whiskey a day. But Howard claimed he never could count very well and that sometimes he got mixed up and that one drink turned into four. But, hell, I couldn't blame him. Sitting around all day like he was forced to was enough to make anybody crave a drink even if it was just for something to do.

But now he seen he was going to get the straight stuff and he got a mighty big gleam in his eye. He took the glass when I handed it to him and said, "What's the occasion? Tryin' to kill me off?"

"Hell no," I said. "But a man can't make a proper toast with watered whiskey."

"That's a fact," he said. "Now what the thunder are we toasting?"

I clinked my glass with his. I said, "If all goes well you are going to be a grandfather."

"Lord A'mighty!" he said.

We said, "Luck" as was our custom and then knocked them back.

Then he set his glass down and said, "Well, I'll just be damned." He got a satisfied look on his face that I didn't reckon was all due to the whiskey. He said, "Been long enough in coming."

I said, "Hell, the way you keep me busy with this ranch's business I'm surprised I've had the time."

"Pshaw!" he said.

We stood there, kind of enjoying the moment, and then I nodded at the whiskey bottle and said, "You keep on sneaking drinks, you ain't likely to be around for the occasion."

He reared up and said, "Here now! When did I raise you to talk like that?"

I gave him a small smile and said, "Somewhere along the line." Then I set my glass down and said, "Howard, I've got to get to work. I just reckoned you'd want the news."

He said, "Guess it will be a boy?"

I give him a sarcastic look. I said, "Sure, Howard, and I've gone into the gypsy business."

Then I turned out of the house and went to looking for our foreman, Harley. It was early spring in the year of 1898 and we were coming into a swift calf crop after an unusually mild winter. We were about to have calves dropping all over the place, and with the quality of our crossbred beef, we couldn't afford to lose a one.

On the way across the ranch yard my youngest brother, Ben, came riding up. He was on a little prancing chestnut that wouldn't stay still while he was trying to talk to me. I knew he was schooling the little filly, but I said, a little impatiently, "Ben, either ride on off and talk to me later or make that damn horse stand. I can't catch but every other word."

Ben said, mildly, "Hell, don't get agitated. I just wanted to give you a piece of news you might be interested in."

I said, "All right, what is this piece of news?"

"One of the hands drifting the Shorthorn herd got sent back to the barn to pick up some stuff for Harley. He said he seen Lew Vara heading this way."

I was standing up near his horse. The animal had been worked pretty hard, and you could take the horse smell right up your nose off him. I said, "Well, okay. So the sheriff is coming. What you reckon we ought to do, get him a cake baked?"

He give me one of his sardonic looks. Ben and I were so much alike it was awful to contemplate. Only difference between us was that I was a good deal wiser and less hotheaded and he was an even size smaller than me. He said, "I reckon he'd rather have whiskey."

I said, "I got some news for you but I ain't going to tell you now."

"What is it?"

I wasn't about to tell him he might be an uncle under such circumstances. I gave his horse a whack on the rump and said, as he went off, "Tell you this evening after work. Now get, and tell Ray Hays I want to see him later on."

He rode off, and I walked back to the ranch house thinking about Lew Vara. Lew, outside of my family, was about the best friend I'd ever had. We'd started off, however in a kind of peculiar way to make friends. Some eight or nine years past Lew and I had had about the worst fistfight I'd ever been in. It occurred at Crook's Saloon and Cafe in Blessing, the closest town to our ranch, about seven miles away, of which we owned a good part. The fight took nearly half an hour, and we both did our dead level best to beat the other to death. I won the fight, but unfairly. Lew had had me down on the saloon floor and was in the process of finishing me off when my groping hand found a beer mug. I smashed him over the head with it in a last-ditch effort to keep my own head on my shoulders. It sent Lew to the infirmary for quite a long stay; I'd fractured his skull. When he was partially recovered Lew sent word to me that as soon as he was able, he was coming to kill me.

But it never happened. When he was free from medical care Lew took off for the Oklahoma Territory, and I didn't hear another word from him for four years. Next time I saw him he came into that very same saloon. I was sitting at a back table when I saw him come through the door. I eased my right leg forward so as to clear my revolver for a quick draw from the holster. But Lew just came up, stuck out his hand in a friendly gesture, and said he wanted to let bygones be bygones. He offered to buy me a drink, but I had a bottle on the table so I just told him to get himself a glass and take advantage of my hospitality.

Which he did.

After that Lew became a friend of the family and was important in helping the Williams family in about three confrontations where his gun and his savvy did a good deal to turn the tide in our favor. After that we ran him against the incumbent sheriff who we'd come to dislike and no longer trust. Lew had been reluctant at first, but I'd told him that money couldn't buy poverty but it could damn well buy the sheriff's job in Matagorda County. As a result he got elected, and so far as I was concerned, he did an outstanding job of keeping the peace in his territory.

Which wasn't saying a great deal because most of the trouble he had to deal with, outside of helping us, was the occasional Saturday night drunk and the odd Main Street dogfight.

So I walked back to the main ranch house wondering what he wanted. But I also knew that if it was in my power to give, Lew could have it.

I was standing on the porch about five minutes later when he came riding up. I said, "You want to come inside or talk outside?"

He swung off his horse. He said, "Let's get inside."

"You want coffee?"

"I could stand it."

"This going to be serious?"

"Is to me."

"All right."

I led him through the house to the dining room, where we generally, as a family, sat around and talked things out. I said, looking at Lew, "Get started on it."

He wouldn't face me. "Wait until the coffee comes. We can talk then."

About then Buttercup came staggering in with a couple of cups of coffee. It didn't much make any difference about what time of day or night it was, Buttercup might or might not be staggering. He was an old hand of our father's who'd helped to develop the Half-Moon. In his day he'd been about the best horse breaker around, but time and tumbles had taken their toll. But Howard wasn't a man to forget past loyalties so he'd kept Buttercup on as a cook. His real name was Butterfield, but me and my brothers had called him Buttercup, a name he clearly despised, for as long as I could remember. He was easily the best shot with a long-range rifle I'd ever seen. He had an old .50-caliber Sharps buffalo rifle, and even with his old eyes and seemingly unsteady hands he was deadly anywhere up to five hundred yards. On more than one occasion I'd had the benefit of that seemingly ageless ability. Now he set the coffee down for us and give all the indications of making himself at home. I said, "Buttercup, go on back out in the kitchen. This is a private conversation."

I sat. I picked up my coffee cup and blew on it and then took a sip. I said, "Let me have it, Lew."

He looked plain miserable. He said, "Justa, you and your family have done me a world of good. So has the town and the county. I used to be the trash of the alley and y'all helped bring me back from nothing." He looked away. He said, "That's why this is so damn hard."

"What's so damned hard?"

But instead of answering straight out he said, "They is going to be people that don't understand. That's why I want you to have the straight of it."

I said, with a little heat, "Goddamnit, Lew, if you don't tell me what's going on I'm going to stretch you out over that kitchen stove in yonder."

He'd been looking away, but now he brought his gaze back to me and said, "I've got to resign, Justa. As sheriff. And not only that, I got to quit this part of the country."

Thoughts of his past life in the Oklahoma Territory flashed through my mind, when he'd been thought an outlaw and later proved innocent. I thought maybe that old business had come up again and he was going to have to flee for his life and his freedom. I said as much.

He give me a look and then made a short bark that I reckoned he took for a laugh. He said, "Naw, you got it about as backwards as can be. It's got to do with my days in the Oklahoma Territory all right, but it ain't the law. Pretty much the opposite of it. It's the outlaw part that's coming to plague me."

It took some doing, but I finally got the whole story out of him. It seemed that the old gang he'd fallen in with in Oklahoma had got wind of his being the sheriff of Matagorda County. They thought that Lew was still the same young hellion and that they had them a bird nest on the ground, what with him being sheriff and all. They'd sent word that they'd be in town in a few days and they figured to "pick the place clean." And they expected Lew's help.

"How'd you get word?"

Lew said, "Right now they are raising hell in Galveston, but they sent the first robin of spring down to let me know to get the welcome mat rolled out. Some kid about eighteen or nineteen. Thinks he's tough."

"Where's he?"

Lew jerked his head in the general direction of Blessing. "I throwed him in jail."

I said, "You got me confused. How is you quitting going to help the situation? Looks like with no law it would be even worse."

He said, "If I ain't here maybe they won't come. I plan to send the robin back with the message I ain't the sheriff and ain't even in the country. Besides, there's plenty of good men in the county for the job that won't attract the riffraff I seem to have done." He looked down at his coffee as if he was ashamed.

I didn't know what to say for a minute. This didn't sound like the Lew Vara I knew. I understood he wasn't afraid and I understood he thought he was doing what he thought was the best for everyone concerned, but I didn't think he was thinking too straight. I said, "Lew, how many of them is there?"

He said, tiredly, "About eighteen all told. Counting the robin in the jail. But they be a bunch of rough hombres. This town ain't equipped to handle such. Not without a whole lot of folks gettin' hurt. And I won't have that. I figured on an argument from you, Justa, but I ain't going to make no battlefield out of this town. I know this bunch. Or kinds like them." Then he raised his head and give me a hard look. "So I don't want no argument out of you. I come out to tell you what was what because I care about what you might think of me. Don't make me no mind about nobody else but I wanted you to know."

I got up. I said, "Finish your coffee. I got to ride over to my house. I'll be back inside of half an hour. Then we'll go into town and look into this matter."

He said, "Damnit, Justa, I done told you I—"

"Yeah, I know what you told me. I also know it ain't really what you want to do. Now we ain't going to argue and I ain't going to try to tell you what to do, but I am going to ask you to let us look into the situation a little before you light a shuck and go tearing out of here. Now will you wait until I ride over to the house and tell Nora I'm going into town?"

He looked uncomfortable, but, after a moment, he nodded. "All right," he said. "But it ain't going to change my mind none."

I said, "Just go in and visit with Howard until I get back. He don't get much company and even as sorry as you are you're better than nothing."

That at least did make him smile a bit. He sipped at his coffee, and I took out the back door to where my horse was waiting.

Nora met me at the front door when I came into the house. She said, "Well, how did the soon-to-be grandpa take it?"

I said, "Howard? Like to have knocked the heels off his boots. I give him a straight shot of whiskey in celebration. He's so damned tickled I don't reckon he's settled down yet."

"What about the others?"

I said, kind of cautiously, "Well, wasn't nobody else around. Ben's out with the herd and Norris is in Blessing. Naturally Buttercup is drunk."

Meanwhile I was kind of edging my way back toward our bedroom. She followed me. I was at the point of strapping on my gunbelt when she came into the room. She said, "Why are you putting on that gun?"

It was my sidegun, a .42/40-caliber Colts revolver that I'd been carrying for several years. I had two of them, one that I wore and one that I carried in my saddlebags. The gun was a .40-caliber chambered weapon on a .42-caliber frame. The heavier frame gave it a nice feel in the hand with very little barrel deflection, and the .40-caliber slug was big enough to stop anything you could hit solid. It had been good luck for me and the best proof of that was that I was alive.

I said, kind of looking away from her, "Well, I've got to go into town."

"Why do you need your gun to go into town?"

I said, "Hell, Nora, I never go into town without a gun. You know that."

"What are you going into town for?"

I said, "Norris has got some papers for me to sign."

"I thought Norris was already in town. What does he need you to sign anything for?"

I kind of blew up. I said, "Damnit, Nora, what is with all these questions? I've got business. Ain't that good enough for you?"

She give me a cool look. "Yes," she said. "I don't mess in your business. It's only when you try and lie to me. Justa, you are the worst liar in the world."

"All right," I said. "All right. Lew Vara has got some trouble. Nothing serious. I'm going to give him a hand. God knows he's helped us out enough." I could hear her maid, Juanita, banging around in the kitchen. I said, "Look, why don't you get Juanita to hitch up the buggy and you and her go up to the big house and fix us a supper. I'll be back before dark and we'll all eat together and celebrate. What about that?"

She looked at me for a long moment. I could see her thinking about all the possibilities. Finally she said, "Are you going to run a risk on the day I've told you you're going to be a father?"

"Hell no!" I said. "What do you think? I'm going in to use a little influence for Lew's sake. I ain't going to be running any risks."

She made a little motion with her hand. "Then why the gun?"

"Hell, Nora, I don't even ride out into the pasture without a gun. Will you quit plaguing me?"

It took a second, but then her smooth, young face calmed down. She said, "I'm sorry, honey. Go and help Lew if you can. Juanita and I will go up to the big house and I'll personally see to supper. You better be back."

I give her a good, loving kiss and then made my adieus, left the house, and mounted my horse and rode off.

But I rode off with a little guilt nagging at me. I swear, it is hell on a man to answer all the tugs he gets on his sleeve. He gets pulled first one way and then the other. A man damn

near needs to be made out of India rubber to handle all of
them. No, I wasn't riding into no danger that March day, but
if we didn't do something about it, it wouldn't be long before
I would be.

A special offer for people who enjoy reading the best Westerns published today.

WESTERNS!

NO OBLIGATION

Mail the coupon below

To start your subscription and receive 2 FREE WESTERNS, fill out the coupon below and mail it today. We'll send your first shipment which includes 2 FREE BOOKS as soon as we receive it.